MAYABHARATA

Meghnad Desai was born in 1940 in Baroda (now Vadodara), Gujarat. He completed his bachelor's and master's degree in Economics in 1958 and 1960, respectively, from University of Bombay (now Mumbai). He got his PhD from the University of Pennsylvania, Philadelphia, USA, in 1964. He worked as an associate specialist in the Department of Agricultural and Resource Economics, University of California, Berkeley, from September 1963 to July 1965. He joined the Department of Economics at the London School of Economics in September 1965. He has worked as a lecturer (1965–77), senior lecturer (1977–80), reader (1980–83) and professor (1984–2003). Since 2003, he is professor emeritus at London School of Economics.

He was awarded the Pravasi Bharatiya Samman in January 2004 and the Padma Bhushan in 2008. He is also a recipient of the Hind Rattan Award award from the Indian Merchants' Chamber. He is an honorary fellow of the London School of Economics and a Fellow of the Royal Society of Arts.

Meghnad Desai was elevated to a peerage in May 1991 and is now known as Lord Desai of St Clement Danes; he sat as a Labour Peer in the House of Lords until November 2020. Now he is a Crossbench (non-affiliated) Peer. He was a member of the mentor group set up to revive Nalanda University by the Ministry of External Affairs, Government of India, in 2007, and was a member of the governing board of Nalanda University. He is the chairman of the Meghnad Desai Academy of Economics, Mumbai, since June 2015. He is the chairman of the advisory board of the Official Monetary and Financial Institutions Forum. He divides his time between London, Delhi and Goa.

He has written over 25 books, including *Applied Econometrics, Marx's Revenge: The Resurgence of Capitalism and the Death of Statist Socialism, Rethinking Islamism: The Ideology of the New Terror, The Rediscovery of India* and *Nehru's Hero: Dilip Kumar in the Life of India.*

Also by the author

Politic Shock: Trump, Modi, Brexit and the Prospect for Liberal Democracy

The Bombay Plan: Blueprint for Economic Resurgence
(with co-author Sanjaya Baru)

Anamika: A Tale of Desire in a Time of War

MAYABHARATA

The Untold Story behind the Death of Lord Krishna

MEGHNAD DESAI

Meghnad Desai
5/9/22

RUPA

Published by
Rupa Publications India Pvt. Ltd 2022
7/16, Ansari Road, Daryaganj
New Delhi 110002

Sales centres:
Allahabad Bengaluru Chennai
Hyderabad Jaipur Kathmandu
Kolkata Mumbai

ISBN: 978-93-5520-550-6

First impression 2022

10 9 8 7 6 5 4 3 2 1

The moral right of the author has been asserted.

Printed in India

Contents

Introduction

Story behind the Story

Novels do not have prefaces and forewords. In what is one of my favourite novels of all time, *Ulysses*, author James Joyce starts immediately with these words: 'Stately, plump Buck Mulligan…'

Mayabharat is a story that has taken me literally a lifetime to write. Well, not so much in actually writing it, but conceiving the problem which was troubling me. So indulge me and listen.

Many years ago, when I was a young boy of fifteen years or so, I had gone with my parents to my uncle's (my father's younger brother) house in Mumbai for dinner. He owned a spacious flat (by Mumbai's reckoning) in Andheri. Post dinner, as families do, there were a lot of interesting discussions, especially between my father and my uncle, considered to be good raconteurs. It was a lively discussion as we were all dedicated readers.

In the middle of a somewhat interesting discussion on deities, the story of Lord Krishna's death, especially how he died, came up. I could immediately visualize Krishna resting in a forest somewhere and suddenly being shot with an arrow in the foot and dying. The killer was an unknown tribal, and in the version we were discussing, he repented and Krishna forgave him. However, as in any story within Mahabharata, there are many versions. Our discussion solely focused on how the tribal came to be there. The story that he mistook the sole of Krishna's foot for a bird did not sound very convincing. Thus, the next hour was spent speculating on this aspect, before finally hitting the sack at midnight.

I was hooked on this version for the rest of my life. What I thought then, but did not say out loud was, *Did Krishna commit suicide, or did he implore the tribal hunter to do what he did?* The issue, as I saw it, was that how could Krishna be killed by another warrior, and a tribal hunter at that?

The next phase in my quest to find out more about Krishna and the role he played in Mahabharata begins in Berkeley, California, where I was working at my first full-time job with the Department of Agricultural & Resource Economics. Throughout my life, be it as a student or as an academic, wherever I have gone, I have gravitated to the library whenever I have had some spare time. I found the libraries in the US a haven of learning and intellect. It was here, and later in the amazing monuments in the jungles of Guatemala, that I stumbled upon the Maya civilization. None of my history courses had even mentioned the Maya civilization as coextensive with Indian and Chinese civilizations, with which I had made myself familiar during the *Hindi–Chini bhai bhai* (Indians and Chinese are brothers) days.

Superficially, it seemed like there were continuities from India to China and Maya. Thus, I added the Mayans to my bag of concerns to travel with. I was also made aware of the great Chicago project of translating all of Mahabharata into English by a single author, with a proper critical textual apparatus of modern criticism. The scheme produced one or two volumes. While I had read several versions in Gujarati, English and Hindi, I had not read the entire text, let alone in its proper sequence. Never, for example, had I read the 'Adi Parva'.[*] Now I had in my hand an English translation of the 'Adi Parva', beautifully printed and edited, and I read it.

---

[*]First of the eighteen books of Mahabharata.

That again blew my mind because the naga context around which the main narrative is built was never known to me. In some corner of my mind perhaps, I had heard about Janamejaya's *yajna* to kill all Nagas to avenge his father Parikshit's death, but did not realize that it was a key to my lifelong search of what happened to Krishna. The great war of Kurukshetra was just a prelude to the next war of the Kurus, which was fought not among themselves, but their common enemy—the Nagas.

Reading the 'Adi Parva' alone, line by line, in English (with the editor's helpful notes) made the epic a different story. The Mahabharata starts with Janamejaya, the great grandson of Arjuna and the son of Parikshit who has been killed by the sting of Naga Takshak, holding a yajna to kill all Nagas. That told me that though the war of Kurukshetra might have ended after those eighteen days, the war against Nagas was yet to be fought by the Kurus.

Hence, the arrival of Janamejaya and his yajna, where Janamejaya asks Vaishampayan to recount the story of the great war at Kurukshetra that his ancestors had fought. But the story itself is not in the words of Vaishampayan. One more layer is overlaid. It is when Ugrasravas arrives in the Naimisha forest, where another yajna is being undertaken, that the rishis present there ask him to retell the story Vaishmapyan had told at the yajna. So, he repeats word for word what Vaishampayan had recited. The punchline was that Takshaka killing Parikshit had incited a revenge yajna by Janamejaya to annihilate all Nagas.

The story of Mahabharata takes a turn with a multigenerational war in the Aryavarta domain, with the Kurukshetra war being the first instalment in the intra-dynastic dispute to settle legitimacy of succession during which fellow Aryan kings across Northern Aryavarta, from Gandhara to Virata, took sides and all but about ten individuals perished. The late Johannes van Buitenen, the genius editor *The Mahabharata* published by the University of Chicago Press, explains how the battle was about legitimate succession and not simply about truth versus evil.

The mystery around Krishna's death was slowly dissipating. Then the obvious struck me as the essence of the story; it was the dual identity of Takshak—man/naga. Growing up, I would hear the news in India about Nagaland's war for autonomy and about Angami Zapu Phizo (1903–90), the influential Naga leader who led the Nagas in the quest for secession from India. It would not go away. Was there continuity in the wars over millennia?

The next obvious discovery was Maya Danav, the architect who built the palace of illusions, where the Pandavas lived in Indraprastha. Was Maya Danav actually a Mayan? I was off to another link in the chain to solve the riddle of Krishna's death. How did he get to Khandava forest, where he was saved from a fire by Krishna and Arjuna? He could have come via the Atlantic, the Mediterranean or the Arabian Sea. But then, what was he doing on the outskirts of Indraprastha? Why had he come at all? No scholarly commentary I had read on the Mahabharata had bothered to ask these questions. After the Pandavas went into exile, or even before, he disappears from the story—and no one cares.

By the time I was asking myself these questions, I had arrived at the midpoint of my life, which was forty years after that family dinner in Andheri at my uncle's flat.

I had made a career in London, got married and was the father of three children—two girls and a boy. My English wife was happy to leave me alone. We were at the Australian National University for the autumn term of 1984, where I had three libraries to explore. One was for Economics and Econometrics, which helped me earn my bread and butter. There was National Centre for Development Studies for my interests in economic development, India, etc. Then there was a general, open library for all. Here found more books on the Mahabharata.

I was now getting educated through the immensely impressive, mainly American scholarship on the subject. Unfortunately, Johannes van Buitenen was no longer alive. The curse on the translators of the Mahabharata, as was said, was that anyone who would try to translate the epic single-handedly, would die before the task could be completed. But Alf Hiltebeitel became my teacher on the epic. Thus, while he was not concerned with my trivial pursuit of translating, I learnt to read the epic in different ways. (See, in particular, Hiltebeitel's *Rethinking the Mahabharata: A Reader's Guide to the Education of the Dharma King* and then *Freud's Mahabharata*.)

It was in a one-volume account of the story of Mahabharata by another author where I picked up the hint about the episode I have made the cause of crisis in Yudhishthira's post-war rule. It is the idea that the king was supposed to bed virgins in his kingdom if they had no other way to simulate the onset of womanhood. This practice was called *droit de seigneur*. Making it the king's *dharma* added a whole extra dimension to it.

Now, I had a starting point for the dharmic crisis of the post-war Kuru reign. Why and how does Maya fit into this story? What was his place in post-war Hastinapur? So, back to the board.

By now I had acquired lots of incidental knowledge. The reason why Maya had come was so obvious that I could have sacked myself from the job! For Mohenjo-Daro, stupid! The incomparable urban architecture had just been recently discovered for most people of my generation. John Marshall's[*] work was still being absorbed. Nehru had described it in *The Discovery of India*. It had not entered the national imagination as anything but genuinely pre-Aryan. I had been following the language question, which was exciting, as bits here and there promised more. The architectural quality of what was left to be seen was beyond doubt. So Maya Danav was looking for the ruins, which he had heard about at his home in what we know as Central South America.

That settled it. He came from the East, sailing the Pacific through the South Sea islands and somehow got to the other

---

[*]John Marshall was in charge of the archaeological digging that led to the discovery of Mohenjo-Daro ruins.

end. Who brought him and why? It was not getting easier, but at least the options were narrowing.

Time was moving fast. I was already doing enough. Then my chance meeting with Kishwar added many new as well as old interests to my evergrowing bag of concerns. This was a whole new engagement with my more fanciful ideas that Indians and, of course, a source near could see through.

I had known Bibek Debroy as an economist on my previous visits during the new open-economy phase of India following the Rao–Singh reforms (1991). When we met socially again at one of those enjoyable dinner parties out in the open in some part of Lutyens' Delhi, I was astonished to know that he was finishing his translation of the Mahabharata. His wife Suparna expressed some concern about the old curse. I dismissed it saying Bibek would be fine, and so he was.

Now I had a reliable, readable translation of the great text. Having come back to the Mahabharata after a long tour around its ramparts, portcullises and dangerous ditches, some of my settled views were shaken. In the fifties in India, the serious critique of ancient Indian culture mounted by Left intellectuals, especially Damodar Dharmananda Kosambi, commanded great influence. I realized that much had happened since then, with recent research writings of Mahabharata having removed some of the combative renderings of the event. An invitation to give the Kosambi Lecture[*] in Goa gave me a chance to revisit his essay on the Gita. I rejected the view that the great war could not have happened as the population of India and reserves of iron ore available weren't sufficient to have supported the military effort.

I decided that the war happened as described. Obviously, the great epic tales, like all such efforts across cultures, works at various levels of 'truth'. But even otherwise, I had read enough about

---

[*]Kosambi Lectures are delivered by eminent scholars in the social sciences and humanities.

the Marxist method to take the Third International orthodoxy, even at the hands of a master like Kosambi, as anything other than an opinion—which can now be rejected. I said as much in my Visaria Memorial Lecture in Ahmedabad in 2019, where I discussed the Kosambi objection.

What began to come across as novel to me was the absence of a sense of geographical distance in the epic. Kurukshetra seemed right outside the doors of Hastinapur complex, as widows of Kaurava princes suddenly appeared in the story for the first time right after the battle ended. Having arrived in Delhi late in my life, I had always thought that they must be close by. I had also read about the battles of Panipat. By now, I was travelling frequently to Amritsar from Delhi to help Kishwar with her Partition Museum project. Travelling by car on modern highways through Haryana, I could see that Kurukshetra was not next door. Assembling eighteen armies on both sides and having the requisite number of horses, elephants and chariots for eighteen lakh foot soldiers, is somewhat manageable over time. But rushing out post-haste to receive your husbands' bodies? That, for sure, would have taken time, even if they went by chariots.

It was the realization while reading 'Stree Parva' in Debroy's translated work which horrified me. Imagine that no dead bodies—human or animal—had been cleared till the eighteenth day, when the war ended. Not even Abhimanyu's or those of the Kaurava princes.

As I have placed my events after the war, I was free to invent what happened. The epic itself gets involved in the Asvamedha yajna. Thus, I had as much scope as I wished. Therefore, my account of the crisis of young Anuja and the insertion of Maya into the story. That done, the last piece, was Krishna, the original cause of all that had happened.

Here again, the idea of distance helped. Why was Krishna in Hastinapur or Indraprastha, while his kingdom was in Dwarka, miles away? The Mahabharata treats Krishna's shuttling between the two as if it were a suburban commute. Of course, Krishna could. I had accepted that he was allowed all his infinite powers in a straightforward non-magical way. He just was Krishna, sending a direct message to Arjuna, 'Yada yada hee dharmasya*,' when the latter was at a crossroads with regards to the epic battle against the Kauravas. Vyasa was another giant who could perform miracles.

The story of the departure of Krishna from north-central India to the Saurashtra sea coast in Dwarka was helpful to me. I had been reading up about why the Indus-Saraswati Valley civilization ended. None of the stories of the Aryan invasion made much sense. Having lived in England since 1965, I at least knew English history was full of stories of invaders—Vikings, Angles, Jutes, Romans and Normans. It took England, which is a part of an archipelago at the farther end of the North Sea and insignificant in size compared to Finland or Sweden, an entire millennium to acquire a distinct identity.

That was when the Normans conquered it in 1066 and joined it to the Eurasian landmass. By this time, India was in midst of its third urban revolution! So, there was no reason to drag in the pastoral migration of Aryan hordes singing their hymns into some blood-curdling invasion.

Therefore, the issue was not invasion. It was climate change that turned the long slice of the subcontinent around the Indus running north to south, which later at some time in history turned arid. Now I had a proper reason why the Vrishnis were in Gokul during Krishna's childhood and then in Dwarka where their youth self-destructed. There had been two long cross-country migrations in two generations led by Krishna's family. K.M. Munshi, the great Gujarati novelist and politician of some note during the early Nehru government, had written a multivolume book on Krishna avatar. He was not only a master storyteller, but deeply

---

*'Whenever dharma is in eclipse, I take birth.'

knowledgeable about ancient Indian culture. He laid down the ancestry of Krishna and the marriage of his grandfather Shura to a Naga princess. I thus closed the loop.

ॐ

1

The King I

In the evening, he went to the battlefield just as he had every day since the war ended. Even after a fortnight, the effects were visible everywhere. Straggling groups of families—women, old men or children—were still searching for the bodies of their lost brothers, husbands, sons and fathers to cremate. Here and there, smoke could be seen rising from nearby funeral pyres. For the souls to be released, the bodies had to be burnt. There were other bodies still to be claimed, despite vultures asserting their rights as scavengers every day.

The carnage was overwhelming, the stench awful. Fighting it out along the vast plain of Kurukshetra since the last eighteen days, they had been too preoccupied to notice the dead on the ground, with odd limbs severed here and there, the injured horses or even the perished elephants. The battleground was located near Samanthapanchaka, the five lakes of blood, which the angry Brahmin sage Parashuram had gathered from the slaughter of his enemies, the Kshatriyas. Those reeking lakes of blood had been a terrible reminder all along of the enormity of what they had been up to. Now, more Kshatriya blood had been spilled.

Valiant kings and princes, great charioteers and intrepid army generals from the length and breadth of Bharatvarsha had been cremated soon after the war, under his supervision, on sandalwood

fires. But they were just a thousand or so. There were hundreds
of thousands of other soldiers, ordinary men come from near and
far, who had also been slain.

The few whose bodies could be claimed by relatives were
disposed of in the evenings after the battle had ended for the day.
But they were the people from around here. The relatives of those
who had travelled a long distance following the banner of their
kings, were still arriving as news of the complete destruction of
all the armies engaged in the battle spread like wildfire. It had
been a battle of good against evil, fought on the battlefield of
duty—a *dharma-kshetra*, as his old blind uncle, the former king
Dhritarashtra, had called it. How was he to know then that his
sons would perish along with all their royal friends!

Yudhishthira was well aware of the fact that he was lucky
to be alive. It depressed him as much as it relieved him: of the
hundreds of thousands who had battled over those eighteen days,
he was one of only ten men who had survived. This thought
was his constant companion, and especially now, as the evening
approached. Those few survivors had to drive their own horses
now. He was fortunate that his charioteer Indrasena had survived
the battle. For those who had lost their charioteers, it was rather
difficult to find another, given the time and circumstance.

The men were all dead, all except the grandfathers who had
been too weak to fight. He became aware of it the day after
the battle, the day he was anointed as the supreme king. Along
with his four brothers and their mentor Krishna, Yudhishthira was
once again reminded that he had survived the battle. They were
the victors. Their five sons had been treacherously murdered by
Asvatthama, the only surviving, but bitter son of their teacher
Dronacharya. He had come late at night—flouting the rules of
war—when the princes were asleep, having celebrated the end of
the war, and killed them even when the Queen kept reminding
him of his impropriety. She too was scarred. Having got her
revenge after all those years of suffering in exile, piled on top of

public humiliation, what did Draupadi have to look forward to? And, what did he, for that matter, or his four brothers?

This was the question he asked the old man who lay there. Twenty-four days after being struck down, the old man had still not given up. Although lying on a bed of arrows, he still had life left in him. He must have been eighty, if not older. They all called him grandfather, although he was, of course, their great uncle. He was born as Devavrata to Goddess Ganga and King Santanu, and was heir to the throne of Hastinapur. After Goddess Ganga had left, Santanu fell in love with a beautiful woman who rowed her boat up and down the river. She caught fish and enticed men. Santanu was keen to marry her, but she was cunning. 'I will marry you,' she said, 'but only if my children inherit the throne.' Her condition left Santanu in a dilemma, writhing in constant misery. As his son, Devavrata could not bring himself to see his father in such agony, he renounced his claim to the throne to allow his father to remarry. He also took an oath to never marry and produce children. As he undertook this vow and fulfilled it, he was christened as Bhishma, the Resolute One. Over the years, he had lived to see his stepbrother's grandchildren grow up as warriors who were destroyed in the battle. Now, he too had fallen.

Years ago, he had tried to find brides for his half-brothers, having raided a swayamvara, where three sisters, all princesses, were going to choose from among the many kings and princes who had gathered to compete for their favours. He knew then that this was the final deed to fulfil the promise given to his father. Amba, Ambika and Ambalika, the daughters of the King of Kashi, were much sought after, and the gathering was a glittering assembly of many kings from around the country. Bhishma had swooped on the ceremony and abducted the three princesses, fighting off all the angry kings and even the father of the three princesses. Of the three, Amba proved to be adamant. She would not marry his stepbrother. She had earlier set her heart on marrying someone

else, the King of Chedi. But now, she announced, she belonged
to Bhishma, her abductor.

But Bhishma could not marry her, as he tried to explain.
He had promised his father, rather his stepmother, that he would
neither marry nor have any children who could threaten the
right of his stepbrothers and their progeny to the throne. He
would take her to the King of Chedi, he suggested. But then,
why should the King of Chedi have a woman who had been
abducted? If Bhishma would not have her, she said, she would
go off and undergo severe penance till her wish was granted—to
be reborn so she could avenge herself. To fulfil her sole desire
to destroy the one who had wronged her, Amba was reborn as
the half man-half woman, named Shikhandi.

Coming back to the present, Bhishma could sense that the
King was approaching. The dog, who was the King's constant
companion, was barking at the stray dogs gnawing at the animal
and human limbs lying around. This was their daily routine. The
virtuous king was the epigone of the whole clan, always truthful
albeit gullible; always straight in his dealings, yet weak when it
came to facing up to cheats. This made him a sober contrast to
his flamboyant brothers, as his queen never stopped reminding him.

She was a strong and passionate woman; her beauty reminded
the old man of that other headstrong beauty Amba, who became
his nemesis. What would now happen to the Kuru line, whose
succession he had tried to secure generation after generation?

The King could say little about that. He reported on the day's
events. He had tried to restore the kingdom after the bloodshed
of the eighteen-day war, which had devoured everything. There
were no young men left in the kingdom—only women, children
and some feeble old men. He had to restore cultivation and crafts;
there were no charioteers, no bow-makers or arrow smiths, no
one to fashion swords or the mace. Horses were in short supply,
as many had been killed in the battle. Should he travel far and
wide and bring people from other lands to settle in his kingdom?

But how far could he go when the armies of the kingdoms of all around had already perished, with no young men left?

The old man, meanwhile, was getting worried about the lineage. The lineage had started generations before his father, with their illustrious ancestor Kuru, but was now down to these five brothers. Their children had been killed. Was the Kuru line to end? Had Amba been right all along? Did he spill his seed into the ground in vain?

The King was helpless. There was little he could offer by way of hope. Their children had died; they were only boys in any case. In killing them at the end of the war, that mad man Asvatthama had taken revenge for his father's life, a life that had been spent in the royal household as a teacher to the five Pandu brothers and their hundred Kaurava cousins. He had, however, taught them to kill very well. But then he had his own score to settle with his enemy.

'Were there no children?' asked Bhishma

'No Grandfather, they are all dead,' said the King.

Fresh wails and cries could be heard from a group of relatives who had just identified the body of their loved one, as if in response to the answer. They must have known he was dead—their son, father, brother or husband. But seeing the body after days of pecking by vultures and dogs reduced them to tears again. It was usually through their ornaments that their loved ones could identify them. There had been no one to rob the dead. No one had survived to gather the loot and run away. Those who were living did not dare come to the battlefield unless they were searching for their dear ones.

'Uttara,' he said almost as an afterthought.

The old man tried to gather his thoughts. As he lay on his bed of arrows, even thinking was difficult by the end of the day. Who was Uttara? There were so many of these grandchildren and great-grandchildren. Which one was she? A daughter of the Kuru lineage? A widow of one of the princes? He could not recall.

'She is a widow, a young one. Married only three full moons before the battle, to Abhimanyu, who fought so bravely even when he was only sixteen.'

'Which one was he?' The old man muttered almost to himself, trying to harness his memory.

'Arjuna's son, a result of his abduction of Subhadra, Krishna's sister. Uttara has morning sickness. There may be hope. Who knows, she may be with child. The old women are not sure yet. That is our one hope—a slender thread to cling on to the future of the Kuru line.'

'Slender as the thread of my remaining life,' the old man sighed.

Their conversation was at an end. The King could see that the old man was tired. He also knew that he would hang on to his life till there was some news about Uttara and her womb. It seemed as if the old man was unable to release himself from the agony of his present dwindling life till he knew that the Kuru lineage was safe. The King promised to return the next day.

ॐ

2

Draupadi

She woke up in the middle of the night. Who was it beside her? The fragrant breath reminded her. It was Nakula, the second-youngest of the five brothers. Of all the brothers she was wedded to, he was the only gentle one, the most innocent. He wasn't her favourite husband though. She loved Arjuna the most. It was he, after all, who had won her many years ago in that faraway place in the foothills of the snowy mountains. Why had her father even gone through all that trouble? She could have married anyone—a cousin or an uncle or even her brother. It was not forbidden.

She had fond memories of her brother, Dhrishtadhyumna, but he was a baby, given to sulks and vengeful memories. Her father, on the other hand, had ambitions. Not for her, but for himself. He had wanted a big gathering with princes coming from everywhere and seeing his kingdom. She was not the only one to be married, after all. Once the princes came, they did not want to return empty-handed. Her cousins and daughters of the brave generals serving her father would also be seen to.

Arjuna was quite a pauper then, though a prince by the virtue of his birth. Her father wanted to turn him down, but Krishna prevailed. It was his plot in any case. He had put her father up to the idea of that lavish tournament, the contest being that of archery, since he knew how good Arjuna was at it. Arjuna was always masterly, then and even later. Even when he was alone with her, he was always striving to be the master, always on top. It almost did not matter to him whether she was there or not. She had to submit.

Poor Nakula, she thought as she looked at him again. Sweetly asleep. He was her husband only because of their mother's strange injunction—to share the prize won by Arjuna—that the brother's had obeyed. That was who she was, just a prize, a bauble, a thing to share and divide up, a thing to gamble and lose, as they did later.

No, not they. Only the King, the eldest. The one who considered her a part of his duty, like he did with life itself. No joy, no sorrow, no passion. He did his duty by her as he did by those virgins now lining up outside his bedchamber every night. It was his duty to repopulate that which he had destroyed. But what about her? She had lost all her five sons in the battle.

But she had gotten her revenge on the Kauravas, the very people who had won her in the gamble and then humiliated her, at a time when she felt less of a person but more of a woman, afflicted as she was with streaming blood. The beast, Dushasana, had dragged her to the court. Drunk with power, he had tried to strip her of her modesty in front of everyone. How she had clung to each garment, understanding at last but only dimly why Krishna had given her that peculiar many-folded cloth to wear. Layer after layer was stripped off her. Everyone laughing, egging on that beast. The elders sat there, silent, mortified and helpless, letting it all happen. Her five husbands had already lost and she was in hock to the enemy. Luckily, the beast started seeing multiple visions. Had Krishna taken care of that?

She loved Bhima like no other. He fulfilled her every desire. He had drawn the beast's blood in the battle and anointed her with his blood-red hands. She had had to have that blood, for it was in her bloody state that the beast had tried to strip her. Rivers of blood had flown for that. A whole race lay dead.

Even her own five sons, who had known little luxury, brought up in exile, hiding, running away from the enemy's spies. Discovery meant forfeit and more years of exile. But at the end, no kingdom will they inherit. They are dead. They had survived the battle, but then the coward butchered them at night while they were asleep, that too after the battle was long over, after all hostilities should have ceased. That cowardly Asvatthama avenged his father's death. He had called it the King's teachery. Did the King lie? If only that were true. If only he had learned to lie more and protected them against all their lies and treachery.

Not all of them were the King's children anyway. She had borne a child for each one of her five husbands. It was her duty, which she had to perform. Her dharma, as they all told her. She only loved Arjuna, but that was against her duty. Had she said so the day Arjuna took her home, she would have had a happier life. But what was the point of regretting now.

There was no pain, no pleasure left.

Nakula had always tried to please her. He always thought about her, never about himself, when with her. He was the uncomplicated one, but a child. He would make himself fragrant for her and learn the acts of pleasing her. He had no ambition, no desire, except to please her. He had succeeded every time.

But now, even he was weary. He had come to her, but could neither please, nor grieve. All along he had only followed. No deed or misdeed could be put on him. He was the baby of the family. He had tried to keep his three half-brothers and his twin brother happy. Left to himself, he would have composed a treatise on fragrances or on the act of pleasing a woman. But he had to battle alongside the rest of them, fight, drink and gamble, wander in exile and live in discomfort.

She had followed as well, eventually. But, she had stunned the court at the gambling match when she said that the King could not have pledged her in a bet as he had already lost himself and thus had no possessions. So, whose possession was she? Why did she have to be anyone's possession, only an instrument for bringing forth their heirs? She was the first woman in generations of Kurus, who had borne her husbands' children. Her husbands themselves were not the natural progeny of their father, Pandu. Kunti, her mother-in-law, had somehow convinced everyone that she had a boon from the gods, and three of her sons—Yudhishthira, Arjuna and Bhima—were conceived from them. She even donated her boon to her co-wife Madri, who could not bear to remain childless. Her husband could not have helped them beget anyway. He was forbidden the intimate contact ever since he contracted a wasting disease. And indeed, that was how he died. A whiff of spring and he could not contain himself. He mounted his second wife, Nakula and Sahadeva's mother, and that was it.

Now look what effects the battle had borne? What a carnage! All those dead bodies. Among them were her brother, her father and her children. Only her husbands survived—all five of them. Surely not all deserved to live. Sahadeva—the soul tormented with knowledge and curiosity, the one for whom she was just a pillow of comfort—should remain alive. If only she could choose whom to let live and whom to let die.

But she had almost no choice. She had vowed revenge and had got it. To avenge her, rivers of blood had flown. But what good was a cupful of blood, even if she streaked the parting of her hair with it? Could it undo the thirteen years of exile and suffering and now the perpetual grief of losing her children? Who could answer that for her? Not the King; he was so just, he had no doubts. Nor Bhima; doubts would perplex and puzzle him. The twins were too innocent—even Sahadeva with all his knowledge had no understanding. It will have to be Arjuna. Tomorrow will be his night with her. Will he come or will he also be struck by the impotency caused by war? She will have to please him, then maybe he will talk. Oh, how she ached inside! If only Nakula could wake up and fulfil her.

3

Story of the Horse: Asvatthama

He ran and ran and ran, all through the night. It was too dangerous in the daylight. He then hid and slept. But the nights were not long enough, even though he was running north. He had headed for the hills and then beyond to the snow-clad mountains. When he got there, he thought, he would have some peace and perhaps cool off. The wound on his head made him feel feverish and perpetually hot. Was his fever real or was it a curse? He could never be sure, just as he thought that every tree and every creature he passed at night could be a friend or maybe something else in disguise. Could it be that Krishna, that evil black magician, was pursuing him in a different guise every night?

They will come and take revenge. His had been sweet, but not really enough. Though hardly ten had survived, among the survivors were the King and his four brothers and Krishna. Oh, his dear, dear father! A man of learning, teacher to all the princes, those on both sides of the battle. Curse that evil King Drupada. He befriended him when they were students together and stole all his secret knowledge. King Drupada insulted his father and never again was the dear man the same. He vowed revenge, but what good did it do him.

Asvatthama had taken his revenge. But there was so much to

requite, foremost being avenging the wrong done to his father in his youth after which he had suffered penury until the day when the princes—all hundred and five of them—were found in the forest, bewildered and distressed after Duryodhana, the eldest, had dropped his ring down an old well. His father had retrieved it. It was such a simple thing as his father explained to him later. He had knitted a small basket from some grass to hold the ring. He lowered it below the ring and fetched it up. Those stupid warriors. They thought it was a miracle. They hadn't seen any of his real knowledge, his secret strength. Only he, his son, had been taught that. As far as the princes were concerned, he taught them all the superficial things he knew so well—archery, mace, swords, chariot riding. So little, but it meant so much to them. He became rich, being a teacher to all the princes. It was then that Asvatthama's life changed as well. There was enough to eat and there were friends to play with. Although they were princes, not all of them were bad. Only Arjuna was jealous. He wanted to be the best pupil. He wanted to know everything his father had to offer. He was jealous that the son would get some secrets that he, the great Arjuna, would not. He trained all the time. Even at night.

Father taught him how. It was a nice trick. They were all having supper one evening in the tent when his father cleverly snuffed out all the lights. He helped him do that. Pandemonium broke out among the princes as soon as the lights went out, but after a while they continued eating. Only Arjuna got the message. Just as even in the dark your hand knows where your mouth is, your arrow should know its target.

Arjuna was a champion warrior who acquired mastery in archery: by being committed to being on the top; however, he was also jealous of rivals, and even unfair, as was evident when he tried to avoid the archery battle with Karna on the grounds that, while the great Arjuna was a prince, Karna was only a charioteer's son. Duryodhana was delighted then and had grabbed the opportunity. He immediately gave Karna some land and made him a prince. Arjuna refused to fight even then. And in the last battle, they ended up tricking Karna.

They were all tricksters. They cheated all the time and claimed they were wronged. In fact, they had wronged his father. After being his best pupil, Arjuna went and married his enemy's daughter. They all married her. Asvatthama suspected, though, that Krishna had tricked them into that marriage. He had suddenly claimed that he was the evil king's nephew, brother to the evil dark queen who took the five brothers as husbands. He sealed his father's fate then. However, Arjuna claimed that he was unaware of the long-standing enmity between his father and King Drupada. How was he to know the teacher never told him?

There are no bygones. It was again on the battlefield after all these years that his father had to pay for his honesty and his courage. They could never hope to defeat him, not in archery, not in personal combat, not by sword or mace. He wreaked havoc on the battlefield. He knew his enemy's sons were there, so he went for them all. But then Krishna knew his soft spot, a spot which, if used well, could defeat his father. He let the rumours fly: Asvatthama is dead! Asvatthama is dead! As the cry spread, there was consternation. It was early afternoon and yet the battle came to a halt. No one knew what had happened. Was it true? Had the beloved son of Drona the teacher been killed?

Who could believe that fool Bhima? So, his father had asked Yudhishthira, the great upholder of truth and duty. Was it true? Was Asvatthama dead? Yudhishthira knew that the son was not dead; merely drugged and hidden. But there was an elephant of that name on their side and Krishna had him killed deliberately. So Yudhishthira lied. He said, 'Yes, my teacher, it is true that Asvatthama is dead.' There was a stunned silence. As a cry leapt out of Father's throat, Yudhishthira then whispered to himself, 'But I know not whether it's a man or an elephant.'

And that man was now the king, the sole inheritor of the kingdom of the Kurus. The liar, his father's true killer. Poor

Father. He cast away his weapons and let his enemy's son kill him, defenceless. But then Drupada and his son always broke the rules. Cowards. Anyway, now they will cry. He, Asvatthama, would make sure of that. The King might reign, but not his progeny. Even Duryodhana was dead, as were all his brothers and all their sons. So why should the Pandava children live? Asvatthama knew a thing or two, the secrets his father had told him—how to disguise yourself; how to muffle your footsteps; how to strangle before the victim could cry; how to set fire and run away before the flames could catch you.

They were after him for that. The wound to his head had been caused by that evil Krishna—of that he was sure. Asvatthama was sure that it was not the end. Krishna would come one day, disguised as a tiger or an eagle or even a simple beggar, and trick him. Asvatthama had killed five of his nephews, children of his so-called sister. He had made sure that the kingdom would not go to the line of Pandavas. Let vultures eat it away. Let the half-castes pollute their women. Let famine take their land. They had no men left alive in the kingdom, save those five and Krishna. Their women were too old to bear children. The King and his brothers were hardly in the flower of their youth. No, there won't be any children there. Let the kingdom be without a king. Maybe the dark people from beyond the Madra will come and populate it again. They will wipe out every sign of these people: their palaces, their archery, their sacrifices and their poetry.

He will be the only one left. Someone had said Krishna had cursed him to live forever, in perpetual agony. But he must not believe those lies that Krishna spread. He must run and run. He must get to the hills and beyond the hills to the mountains which were cool and high, beyond the reach of Krishna and his black magic. In the end, he was happy that he had won. He had taken his revenge on both these families and on Krishna.

ಬ

4

The Old Man's Story

He was now a very, very old man and on the verge of leaving this world. But, he could not give up just yet, not until he had heard about that young widow and her child. Now, which one was she? The king had said it was Arjuna's son by Subhadra, that bold boy Abhimanyu, who had fought so bravely in the battle. It had taken them a complete encircling strategy to kill him. He was only sixteen. It was his wife, whatever she was called. He could not remember. His bed of arrows hurt again.

He was used to pain. He had learnt self-control early in life, ever since his father had needed his support, many moons ago. His father King Santanu—the great-grandfather of the present king—had fallen in love. Widowed, not quite, but abandoned by his wife, the ever wandering Ganga. After begetting him, Ganga left, never to return. He remembered his mother. She was the most beautiful woman he had ever seen. She had taken him off to heaven, to Indra's court. He had been pampered by those beautiful apsaras who entertained Indra day and night. He grew up amid the gods. Then she had taken him back when he was old enough and handed him over to his father. He could still recall the smell and touch of her body, as she had carried him everywhere when he was growing up, and how she smothered him with kisses! Her long flowing hair, beautiful face and fair skin were the delight of the gods. His mother Ganga was truly divine.

Years after his mother had left, his father had fallen in love with a fisherman's daughter. He was forlorn for many months. He would neither eat, nor attend to his duties. He, a callow youth of fifteen, had to help his father. 'What is it that troubles you, Father? Tell me what I can do to ease your pain. I will do whatever is necessary. I give you my word.' Much persuasion was required before the pining lover admitted that he could not marry his sweetheart unless he promised her that only the children borne out their union, and not he, Devavrata, the eldest son, would get the throne.

'Is that all?' the son asked.

'No, she also wants her children's children to continue to inherit the kingdom.' Her line should prevail forever and ever. Not the line of the wayward first wife, Ganga.

Listening to his father intently, he promised him he would never marry, nor would he ever couple with any woman or take any chance that may lead to the birth of children and rival claims on the Kuru throne. But that was just the negative side of it. His stepmother, the fisherwoman who flaunted the fact that she smelt of freshwater fish, made him do more. His two half-brothers were feeble. They could not do any of the hardy princely things that a scion of the Kuru family should be able to. They could not drive a chariot, nor shoot an arrow. They were too effete to learn sword fighting and too weak to lift a mace. They were indulgent and the chase of palace maids had debilitated them further, and then Chitrangada, the first born of the two, died in his youth.

Matsyagandha (Satyavati), his stepmother, hardly older than him, kept goading him. How was he going to keep his promise to his father, now gone, to continue his line? So Devavrata—now known as Bhishma for his determined sacrifice—thought of a plan.

Blood. There was too much of it in the Kuru line. Children

died young, killed cruelly. He recalled his mother, the wayward Ganga. She had borne his father eight sons, but the first seven had been put to death by her upon their birth. His father could only watch in horror. He had given her his word not to question her actions. She was a mystery, an enigma. Santanu did not know whence she derived the power she had over him and over everyone else. But when the last child was born and Ganga took him down to the river, he could bear no longer.

'Stop,' he said. 'Why do you kill all my sons?'

She smiled and said, 'This is the end then. You promised never to ask, but now you have done as I expected. Today, I will tell you all about myself. I am Ganga, Siva's daughter, his protégée. All the babies I have killed were heavenly creatures, cursed to spend only a little time on earth. I merely helped shorten their stay. But this is my favourite son and I will return him to you one day. Goodbye.'

ᔑ

Uttara. That was her name. That young girl who may be with child. He now remembered, though he could not recall which one she was. He never could look these young girls in the eye. It did not get any easier, no matter how old he got. Long ago, when they stripped Draupadi in court, he merely sat there, confused and utterly embarrassed. He had never stopped feeling the pang though. Now, on his deathbed, his mind was full of visions of Amba. They mingled with the faint smell of his mother. Was it her? Maybe it was one of the apsaras who had carried him around in Indra's palace. Who could tell?

He should have reneged on his promise and sported himself with all the young princesses and the palace maids, just like Krishna, who had managed all his life enticing, attracting and seducing women. He had eight wives and scores of lovers, but somehow only one son each from just the two of them. How did he manage, only he knew! Perhaps he had the right idea. Why strive after progeny if it was all to come to a naught? One may as well spill one's seed in barren women as in the barren earth.

It was getting dark now. The jackals were howling even more frequently. Despite being prostrate on his bed of arrows, Bhishma could sense the glow of fires all around him. He must live on. He must know. Will she have a son?

ನಲ

5

The Arjuna Story

She lay there waiting for Arjuna to come. It had been a long time, since before the battle. The eve of the battle had been his night with her, but he had not been himself at all. He was perplexed and fidgety. He had been perfunctory with her, taking her in his arms, but muttering about death and destruction. She had got herself bathed and perfumed and had gone to great lengths to be desirable for him, but had failed.

She had once known how to be desirable. She had to, with five husbands and with each in his own ways. She knew who liked what. With the king it was straightforward; he saw it as his duty. It was a simple matter, a task to be performed, a task that was expected of him and of her to produce an heir. Nakula, well, he wanted to please her. He would go to any lengths to make sure that she was happy. He would devise new ways to satisfy her. Sahadeva was broody; if he was happy with his thoughts, he would be pleasant. But then he was always with his thoughts, very rarely with her. Bhima was simple. For him it was like having a meal. But Arjuna, he was different. You could never be sure what fancy would take him. If he was into himself, she was his slave and had to do exactly what he wanted. But then there were nights when he was all solicitous and wanted to be her slave. But this was harder because she had to do all the thinking and the work. She had to show that she was being pleasured.

He liked the fragrance of sandalwood and the aroma of marigold petals strewn on the bed. She laid aside some *soma* just in case he wanted to slip into oblivion as much as she did. There had been times when he had come to her, preoccupied with another—Subhadra or Ulupi or someone—he had met on his travels. They had given him different joys. She was competing with unknown rivals, undiscovered spectres. She looked at her dark body, still supple and glowing after her bath. She pinched herself to make her charms even more obvious. She was now perfumed all over, every part anointed. She made sure the earthen lamp had enough oil. She wanted him to see her again after all these days, draped in a single garment, ready for him. Her hunger was absolute. It could not be assuaged, neither by the king, nor Nakula, though he did his best. It had to be Arjuna.

She knew he had gone to visit Uttara, his bereaved daughter-in-law. Would that make him think of Subhadra, that cowherd? Though she maybe a princess, she reeked of cow dung. How could Arjuna have done that, after but one year of marriage? True, she was not the wife he had won in the contest. True, he had to share her with all his brothers, but was that her fault? All she had wanted was him. She spread herself unconsciously as she thought about him. Oh, why wouldn't he come?

The soma was soothing, but then it also let her mind run loose. Krishna claimed to be her brother, but it was Subhadra who was his blood sister. Was plotting her abduction in cohort with Arjuna, who was smitten with her, a strategy on Krishna's part? He did succeed, and now it was his sister's daughter-in-law who carried all the hopes of the line… Uttara was young and fertile. Before he was killed, Abhimanyu had planted his seed inside her. Will she bear a son and will that son inherit the kingdom which rightfully belonged to her sons, who were now dead? But no, she could still bear children. It had been done before. She was not old yet; she felt her insides get warm and wet at the thought.

He came in, and bowed down in thought, muttering to himself. She poured him some soma. It was warm, but he gulped it down, hardly thinking what he was doing. 'It has been a hard battle. You need more. It is time to relax now,' she said.

He gulped it down again. It must have burnt his throat. He coughed. She knew he was beside himself and wanted to be in a state of oblivion. If that was what he wanted, she would give him that. She refilled his cup. He started swallowing again and, suddenly, for the first time that night, looked at her as if she were a stranger. Fair enough, a stranger she will be.

'Come then, prince. You hardly know me, but I can quench your thirst.' He seemed interested, so she continued. 'Prince, now that you have asked for a stranger tonight, did I please you?'

She slid past him, making sure he touched her, and shut the door behind. She then came back again rubbing herself against him. 'Drink,' she said. I am here to help you forget. Did he know where he was? Did he like the game? Was he remembering this is how she played with him before?

She didn't care. She let her garments slip and turned around pretending to be gazing at herself in the mirror. She felt him behind her, closer now. He cupped her breasts in his hands as it often pleased him to do. She knew then that the game was on. She moaned. 'What are you doing to me, prince? I am just an ordinary housewife in your town. They said they will take my husband away if I did not come here. Please let me go.'

But it seemed as if he wasn't there, even though he was. He was somewhere else. She persisted for a while, but he turned away, limp and cold.

Though in utter despair, Draupadi did not cry, neither for herself, nor for him. He was lost, he wasn't there. He was not her brave Arjuna, who could keep her awake all night and still be not replete. He was neither the torturer, nor the master pleasurer she knew so well.

But she still had time. They had hardly been together. She

led him to the bed and sat him down. They did not speak for a while. She stroked his head gently. Soon he was lying with his head in her lap and she continued to gently massage his temple. He was beginning to relax, though every now and then he jerked as if caught in a spasm. 'How could we do it?' he said, suddenly sitting up. 'What utter, utter folly! What have we gained from it?'

'We did it, my love, because we had nothing left to lose. We did it because of all the insults and humiliations and wanderings we had to suffer. We did it because I had a burning desire in me for all those years to avenge myself against all those cousins of yours who ravaged me in front of the entire court and against all the uncles, the great uncles and the elders who looked on silently, while I stood there, my blood dripping. I was brought before them, stripped and grabbed at. I wanted it done not for your kingdom or for your land or for the animals, but for my own humiliated self.'

'So, are you happy now?'

'I was for a while, that brief moment when Bhima brought me Dushashan's blood cupped in his hands and smeared my hair with it. I wanted that to put my fire out, to put one fire out and to rekindle the desire to feel my body as my own again, to be able to live and give as I wanted to. I was made whole again when I smelled that fresh blood on Bhima's hand.'

He looked at her, surprised at her anguish. He had forgotten how she had borne that humiliation for all these years. In the aftermath of the insults that the brothers had felt at their defeat in the dice game and the ensuing loss of their wealth, they would often forget her hurt. She had refused to comb her hair or tie it or put any decoration in it for all these thirteen years. She had followed her husbands, obeyed them, served them and even cheered them up. But she could never be cheerful herself anymore. The joyous, sensuous girl he had won for himself all those many years ago had grown into a hard woman. Only now she had begun to evince a spark.

He kissed her deeply this time, like he used to years ago. He was surprised, thrilled and puzzled at her ardent response. There was a resurgence of joy in her coupled with a manic desperation and the fear that he would drop her. He held her close to him and could feel her heart beating very fast.

'No, I am not happy, Arjuna. Not since that beast Asvatthama killed my children. My happiness lasted but a twilight. I want them again. I want your children, Arjuna. I am young enough, and now I shall leave behind all pretence that I love all your brothers equally. I can no longer believe it is my station in life, my dharma, to love you all equally. I cannot do it. I have seen enough canons of duty flouted by the King and by you and Krishna. I will not be the only one left performing my duty. It is you who won me and it is your children that I want. Maybe only one, be it a daughter. It would suffice for me. I want something of you and me to last, to laugh at all the dead who laughed at me while they were alive. I will now only consort with you, Arjuna. Hold me. Don't abandon me as you did before.'

Arjuna held her as close as he could, but his kiss now had infinite sadness. He held her mouth for long and then kissed the nape of her neck. But she knew that he was holding her off without telling her so, not rejecting her so much as not giving her the go ahead. He sighed.

'How can I bring anything new into this world, Draupadi? I, who destroyed so much. I could have let them all live and perhaps we could have settled amicably, far away from Hastinapur, far from those poisonous Kauravas. We could have built another kingdom, like we did before. But now we have killed all before us and ones who we did not kill have been killed by our enemies. Have you seen Hastinapur? There is not a man left between the age of fourteen and sixty. There are women everywhere, widowed, fatherless and childless, without their betrothed, their lovers. The King will have to perform his duty to beget children with the virgins. But then what? What is their life beyond that one night with him? Who will be the real father to their children, laugh with them and play with them, teach them to shoot arrows, play marbles? What a waste of womanhood, of manhood, of the world.'

'But Arjuna, my love, my prince! You knew all this before. I remember the night before the battle. You were agitated and unhappy then. I could not hold you in my arms for a second, nor tell you how much I wanted you to go and fight out there. You were refusing to fight, but then you went out and came back late, almost towards the morning. You laid beside me and even before I could stir, you took me in the same triumphant way that you used to. I knew, half awake, half asleep, but ecstatically happy, lying there beneath you, that my love had returned. You were my brave warrior again. What has happened then? And where is my brave warrior now?'

'The night before the battle was the strangest night of my life. Even now when I think about it, I cannot fathom what happened. It is even harder to make sense of it now, but then I was in a trance.'

He shivered as he thought about it. She held him closer, but was aware that he was already shrinking into himself. She rubbed her face against his arms, encouraging him to go on.

'For days before, I had plotted many moves, encirclements and attacks. I had remembered all I had known about the strengths and weaknesses of Bhishma, Drona and Karna. I knew how I would position our brave partners and my brothers in the battlefield. This was to be my greatest moment and I had prepared for it all my life. As the day neared its end, I was exhausted but still full of spirit. I walked out of my tent at twilight and went to look at the kurukshetra itself. The more I looked, the more troubled I became.

In the fading light, I began to see visions of mangled bodies, of dying friends, of those too old to resist and others too young to defend themselves. Cries began to fill my ears and my feet began to feel heavy, as if stuck in the ground, muddy with blood.

I began to smell rotting flesh of horses and elephants, of dogs pecked by vultures, of rats running all over the dead. I was chilled. At first, I could hardly move to turn around. When I finally did, I knew that I didn't want to fight, even if it meant the possession of the earth itself. Nothing pleased me and none could speak to me.

The King was so surprised he could not even begin to argue. Bhima was beside himself with rage. He pushed me in your direction, hoping you would rekindle the fire that had gone out. But you saw me. There was nothing that could move me. As I walked out of your tent, I thought of killing myself before the battle began at dawn. But then I saw the light still burning inside Krishna's tent. He of all people, I thought, would understand my pain. He would settle it all, at the last minute, by some clever device, some subtle compromise. He would, even then, have a treaty worked out that would satisfy everyone, avert the war and save us all.

I went in the tent and poured my heart out to Krishna. I did not want to kill my cousins, my grandfather, my teacher, I told him. He smiled and sat me down. He brought me a drink of milk. He said it would soothe me. Then he took me in the chariot he was to drive for me. We went to the battlefield. He placed the chariot where I was going to be positioned the following day. I could see a field packed with all the warriors— Duryodhana, Bhishma, Drona and hundreds of soldiers across. Then, I saw the people on my side. I was even more upset then. My bow, the *gandiva,* slipped out of my hands and I slumped down in the chariot. I do not know how long I talked for with him. Sometimes it feels like it was several days and nights. At other times, it all goes by in a flash. Even now I cannot not tell you how long it was.'

Draupadi softly said, 'Nor can I, Arjuna, nor can I. But I do know that you came back to me later that night. I do not know how long I had been asleep for or even if I had slept at all. When you walked out, at first, I had the worst fear of my life. I did not wish to talk to any of my other husbands. So I stayed in and blew out my lamp. When you came back, you did not need any lamp. You were glowing with a strange heat, such as I had never felt before. You took me in ways which were long forgotten, if there ever were such ways. I was thrilled and scared and worn out by the time dawn came. You then got up and went to the battle as if nothing had ever worried you.'

'All I remember is that Krishna just smiled and dismissed my fears. He said I was tired and tense. He asked if had I not gotten any comfort from you. If not, he asked, could he put my mind at rest and tell me that I was merely being childish and cowardly?

He said I must have been beyond cure. Krishna had some marvellous arguments on why I was wrong. He spoke about the need to act and the need to know, but the one thing I remember was him saying that I had to know him and be devoted to him. I must have said something, asked him a question. Because I remember how he suddenly seemed to expand before my eyes and fill the entire sky. He seemed to fill the space around him. I could see the sky, but with a thousand suns shining, dazzling, but not frightening.

He seemed to have the entire battle, which was yet to come, conjured up in the palm of his hand. We were all there. I could even see myself. That vision of Krishna filling the space around him and reaching up to the sky may have been a dream, but I recall it vividly. Had I fallen asleep or had he conjured up one of his many miracles, I will never know. The battle ahead, all of us—uncles, brothers, cousins, nephews, in-laws and wives—seemed puny and pointless. The battle was like a twinkle in his eyes. How it was and why it was, I do not know. I do not recall anything after that.'

'Not even coming to me?'

'No, my love, not even that. I recall that there was a different fragrance; it was not your usual one. You, I remember as a mixture of many colours. I recall music in my ears and, yes, the fragrance. But no touch, no speech.'

'O, Arjuna!'

'All I remember is the conch announcing the dawn. It was then that I realized I was lying beside you. You were deep in thought or blissfully lost in some dream. I left you knowing that all I had to do was win the battle. I knew I was going to win. I was happy with my task.'

'So when did it end?'

'I was happy enough to begin. But as Bhishma died, I began to think that killing him, especially in the peculiar way in which Shikhandi did, was not right.'

'But he isn't dead yet.'

'Yes, I know. But isn't that as much a delusion as everything else in our lives? As I made him a bed of arrows to lie on, I began to envy him. He was free from any further care or worry. But I also knew that he had failed to achieve what he most wanted. He gave up everything so that the Kuru line would continue, but then it did not, did it?'

'Why do you say so?'

'He gave up his claim to the throne and any desire for women so that his half-brothers' line could continue. But they didn't have any children. My father and Dhritarashtra were, after all, the children of Vyasa, called in especially to continue the line. Nor did my father have any children.'

'What do you mean?'

'You know the story. My mother got us as a boon from the gods. It was such a shock to learn that Karna was my elder brother. Indeed, he should have been the king, but he was abandoned early by her as she was unmarried at the time he was born. The twins Nakula and Sahadeva are also god's gifts. Yes, I gave you our child and so did all my brothers, but fate did not will that we have surviving children in the Kuru line.

Our children are all dead. Duryodhana and all his brothers

are dead, as are their children. No one in the Kuru line is left. All we have left is Uttara, and who knows if she or her child will survive?'

Draupadi looked up at Arjuna. His face was pale. He looked infinitely tired. She stroked his head and gently kissed him. Her whole being was crying out to say, *I will give you a child again! With you, tonight, I can continue the Kuru line. Take me, Arjuna. Maybe not for myself, not for love, not even for desire, but for your future line.* But she knew it was not the time. She laid his head down, resting it on a pillow and got up to fill his cup again. As she walked away from him, she was conscious of his eyes on her. She was aware that her supple dark body was still attractive. She had all the hope for the future.

When she gave him his cup again, he took a sip and then put his arms around her. No, not yet. He wasn't ready. She began to rub him gently, to relax him again, so he would be the man she so deeply desired. But that was not to be yet. He sat up with a start.

'When Abhimanyu died...' His voice broke down. She gave him his cup and he took a few sips, but coughed as the soma burnt his throat.

'When Abhimanyu died,' he resumed, 'I could not think of anything at all. I had been diverted from the main battle and that is when they tricked him. I had taught him the encircling strategy, but only half of it. He had yet to learn how to close in on the enemy and escape. He went to fight inside the chakravyuh, but couldn't get out. As I sat that evening with his head in my lap, I tried to recall what Krishna had said the other night about bhakti and karma, about the utter irrelevance of individual human life, of the pride of self. But I could not recall a single word. I could not even conjure up the great vision I had seen. I could only think of the many ways in which I could have saved my son had I been there. I plotted and replotted every move. But what was the use? What I had learnt from Krishna seemed futile.

What mattered was my son, who was not there anymore.'

She said, 'I could never understand Krishna. I do not even know now what makes him do and say what he does. He has a design for everything and everyone, but it is not for me to know what it is. He says he is my brother, but then he is not like Dhrishtadhyumna. He was my brother. He was someone I could argue with, someone I could love, someone I could hate. But Krishna I can only admire and worship, and wonder what he will be up to next.'

'But he has been your protector. Remember that time in the court?'

'How could I ever forget? Back then he saved me, but why did he not help you all? Why did he not stop the gambling before it got that far? Why wait to save me until after I had been dragged there, wet with my own blood, naked except for a single piece of cloth?'

'Maybe we are not meant to understand. We just have to trust him. That night before the battle he kept on saying, "Leave everything to me."'

'So you did, and what are we left with now? He has everything. He has not lost his son, nor has he lost a brother or a cousin. His wives are many and they all await him eagerly every night. And here I am. I have lost my children, my father, my brother.

'*Our* children. They were mine as well.'

'Yes, and your uncles and your brother Karna, your teacher Drona. Your grandfather, Bhishma.'

He saw the sadness and the anger in her eyes. It was as if he had transferred his sorrow to her. He did not want her to be desolate.

'You had your revenge though. And we have our kingdom now.' He drew her closer.

'But I lost my children the same day I got my revenge. It is all the same to Krishna. He can take away with one hand what he gives with the other. I cannot fathom what he said to you, but to me it seems it cannot be the way. You fight and kill and love, but if it is not really you who is doing this, what then is the point of life? It feels as if Abhimanyu is here, but he is not here. Maybe in Krishna's eyes I am nothing and you are nothing, but for me you are what I want. Even if it is all illusion, *maya*. I would rather have Abhimanyu alive as maya than dead.'

He could only look at her. He had been struggling with his thoughts ever since the battle ended, if not before. He had been hit by so much. The conversation with Krishna was like some eternal dream. It kept coming back to him, but he never succeeded in grasping it. The battle had been a hard one. Physically, he was tired, and the exultation of victory was gone. All those deaths had worn him down. He had come to her tonight, drained of desire, but now there she was. She had made sense of everything in her own simple way.

At least she knew what she could grasp and so did not let it go. He lifted her face to his and started gently kissing her. Her eyes were fiery at first, black as the hair that was now draping her shoulders. He went slowly at first, but then rapidly kissed her cheeks, her brow, her ears, her chin and finally her mouth. He had known her all these years and she could still surprise him—as she did tonight.

She lay him down beside her and soon they were lost in each other. She said, 'I am life. I am not maya. I create life. I will not be defeated. They can kill all, all, but I am a woman. I can give birth again. We can give birth again. We can create something where there was nothing before.'

He looked up at her. She was now like a vision. Her long black hair all around her, flying as she went up and down. She was laughing.

'Come, my warrior. You won me as you shot an arrow in the eye of that fish rotating on the ceiling of that room. I was watching you. You know you hit the mark. I am that fish and that eye of the fish where you have your arrow. And all the other kings and princes and noblemen are dust. They are all gone, but you are still here. There is no dividing us now.' She continued, 'I am life and I will give life. We will win again, my brave archer. Leave it all to me. I am your woman. I am the woman. I am you and there is no one else. There is no death, only life.'

ৎৄৎ

6

The King's Predicament

The King was nonplussed. The virgin lay on the shiny marble floor of his bedroom, rigid and unconscious. Her nakedness was cold and off-putting. At the best of times, Yudhishthira had an aversion to physical love beyond what his duty demanded. Only Draupadi had made it tolerable. She soothed him without being demanding. Now the burden of kingship demanded that he provide for the women he has rendered fatherless, husbandless, and especially those without a prospect of finding an unmarried man to deflower them. Only a king could bed a virgin while being married.

Yudhishthira was now in a state of panic. He surely could not send the girl back intact; he would have failed in his duty as a king, and his duty meant more to him than anything else. But the body in his bedroom was hardly calling him to do his duty.

This virgin was younger than the many others he had taken since he became king again. She was like a delicate flower, or a frightened gazelle. She came in what her mother must have thought was a dress that makes her look attractive. Even then, her young body with breasts barely budding and her shoulders hunched with embarrassment, did not invite attention. The king welcomed her and bade her sit down on the bed. He asked her name.

'Anuja,' she faintly muttered. The king began to caress her, thinking all the time of Draupadi. Anuja froze as he touched her. The king persisted, for he had to do his duty. He began to slide her clothes off. Anuja did not know what to do. She stood up, exposing herself to the king, as if making it easier for him to unclothe her. The king again thought of Draupadi, but this time all he could visualize was Draupadi at the court after they had lost the gamble, with Dushasana dragging her in front of everyone.

Anuja moved closer to the king, as if prepared for the experience. She sat on his lap as she had been tutored by her mother, who had taught her how men could be pleased. The King was petrified. He was just braving himself to take this virgin, but his mind was fixated on Draupadi being disrobed. Anuja began to caress him as she had been instructed. The King looked at her and responded. She was cheered.

'How can I please my lord? Shall I sing? Shall I massage your feet?'

The King did not know what to say. The girl moved closer to him, took his hands and placed them on her shoulders, while he sat on the bed. She was hoping he would like her. The King decided that he had to get out of his thoughts about Draupadi and deal with this young woman. He drew her closer to him and began playing with her breasts. She had been told what might happen next. She dropped her clothes and lay down on the bed expecting him to force himself upon her. He disrobed himself. He took another gulp of the soma and mounted her.

She did not resist him, but did not help him either. She had been told this may happen, but not what she was to do. She shut her eyes, waiting for the royal assault. Minutes passed and the King tried and tried, but failed to take her. She opened her eyes and found that he had abandoned her. He was standing naked and was flaccid. The sight of the old body with its wrinkled skin, stooping back and a white shrunken penis bewildered her. Anuja gasped and got off the bed, but fainted.

He immediately thought of Draupadi. She was worldly-wise in such matters. But she was with another, and by a long-standing arrangement, one brother could not intrude when she was with another. Brave as he was, Arjuna was no good in advising him about anything other than war. His younger brothers were ruled out too. Then there was Krishna, he suddenly thought. He was still there. He was to leave for Dwarka the next day, but tonight he was in another part of the palace. And Krishna was a king unlike any of his brothers. Indeed, apart from him, Krishna was the only king alive as far as he knew. Krishna could solve his difficulty in more ways than one.

The king took off his upper garment and draped it over the naked body of the girl. He stepped out of his room. The woman guarding the door was puzzled, wondering how it was all over so soon. She made as if to go in and get the initiate of the evening. The King gestured her to wait. He was going to talk to Krishna, he said. The woman nodded; she might have smirked as he left, but the King was too preoccupied to care.

ॐ

7

Krishna Leela

Krishna was restless in his palace quarters. The war had been exhausting. Eighteen days had taken a toll. His entire army, which he had offered to Duryodhana, was gone. Balarama had walked away in disgust. He could see the sadness in the eyes of the Pandavas, even though they had won the war. Arjuna was beside himself with remorse. He blamed himself for the defeat of his cousins. Nothing Krishna said would persuade him to think otherwise, it happened as it was meant to be. He was still mourning the tragic loss of his son, Abhimanyu and, of course, their guru Drona. He did not have the heart to visit Bhishma. He left that to Yudhishthira.

It was solely on the basis of the strategies concocted by Krishna that Arjuna and his brothers could win the battle. It was meant to be a joyous moment of celebration. But tonight he was restless. He had begun to doubt whether it could all have been different. He did not expect this onslaught of self-doubt. Had he done enough to mediate and settle the dispute? Could he have been kinder to Duryodhana? Should he have kept talking and not displayed his *virata* form in the face of Duryodhana's arrogance?

A hundred doubts crept up in his mind. Maybe he was just lonely, missing his lovely Rukmini and Satyabhama and the many others waiting for him back in Dwarka. He was to leave tomorrow and soon would be nestling in warm embraces and willing submission. They were ever so inventive in finding new ways of pleasing him. Neither could he ever get tired of them, nor they of him. Even after all these years of lovemaking, he knew that when he reached Dwarka, they would make him forget all his woes.

There was a gentle knock on the door. It was the back door, not the front, and hardly audible. But Krishna knew it was someone who, though hesitant to knock, was eager to see him. He opened the door. There, before him, was a woman wrapped in a dark black garment, almost like a shroud. Her face was wrinkled, but her eyes sparkled. Krishna was surprised. This was one woman he did not expect to see.

He said, 'Radha, what brings you here so late?'

'Have you forgotten we always used to meet late at night? You left me waiting for you till the last, after you had sported with those worthless younger ones in Gokul.'

'All these years and you still remember! Come and sit down. What a charming surprise.'

'Why should I sit down? Have you stopped loving me? I do not sit down with you. Take me like you used to, close to your beating heart and wrapped in your strong arms.'

Krishna was overcome with love. How many years ago had he sported with Radha on the banks of Kalindi River? How they used to canoodle late at night, almost close to dawn. She was special. His favourite. His teacher in the art of lovemaking. She was older and ravishingly beautiful. As they lay close again now, Krishna gazed deep at her lovely face, now older and wrinkled, but still dazzling. Several kisses later, they were still closely intertwined. Radha started sobbing. Krishna understood her sorrow. He held her tighter. She separated herself from him, but not before kissing him full on the mouth. To Krishna's surprise, she shed her dark outer garment and continued to undress. She came back to his arms with her lovely form on display for him. He felt the old magic again as he brought her closer to him.

Krishna gently asked, 'What has brought you to Hastinapur from Gokul?'

Radha, her eyes sparkling with tears, said, 'You left us in Gokul to fulfil your mission as Guru Sandipani told you. You never came back. Ayyan was in Kamsa's army. After you killed Kamsa, we settled down and had a son Sudhanva. He was all I had after Ayyan passed away. He was fighting on Duryodhana's side. He died along with all the others. So I came to find his body. I thought you could tell me where to find him. You know everything and did everything in the war.'

Krishna was moved, something he had not felt ever before in his life. He had not felt any personal attachment to the death and destruction caused by the war. But now he felt his heart beat faster. What was he to say to Radha?

Suddenly, a gong sounded; Krishna knew at once that he had a visitor.

Radha sat up suddenly. She separated herself from Krishna. 'They are calling you away from me once again. The whole world needs you. Go. I have had my few moments.'

Before Krishna could stop her, Radha wrapped herself in her garments and left as she had come. Krishna sighed. He had to deal with the burning world, leaving his own desires behind.

ဢ

8

Leave All Things to Me

The King was standing outside, somehow looking older, smaller in stature and diminished. He was about to apologize for the interruption when Krishna put him at ease. 'You should have summoned me, Dharmaraja; in Hastinapur, you command us all!'

'I would never dare to command you, my lord. But I have a dilemma only you can solve.'

'What is it?'

The King explained the problem. He had failed to bed the virgin sent to his chamber. He had failed in his duty as a king.

'But how can I help?'

'You know all, my lord. The virgin must have a royal master before the night is over, otherwise ill luck will befall this kingdom. We have brought enough misery to this land, we have to find a way to prevent this.'

'What do you suggest, O King?'

'Beside me, you are the only reigning king in Hastinapur. Dhritarashtra is too old and blind; my brothers are but princes. Only an anointed king has the right to bed a virgin if there is no hope of her marrying young. You know how I have performed my duty these past many days, but now I stand defeated.'

'Why?'

'As she came to me tonight in her nakedness, all I could think of was the field where the dead lay unburied. Somewhere among the dead was the young man who should have been her joy, not the king who has caused the killing.'

'It is a folly, as you know, to believe that you caused the killing. It is worse. It is egotistical and you, Dharmaraja, have never been known to share that weakness with your younger brothers. Before the battle, I had to cure Arjuna of this malady. Perhaps I should do the same with you.'

'The inspiration you gave to Arjuna on the eve of the battle made us victorious, but, my lord, this is not the hour for fine philosophical argument. We need to rescue the maiden and the kingdom. You are the other king. I request you to take over this burden from my shoulders tonight.'

'You are wrong, Dharmaraja. I am not the only other king in Hastinapur.'

'Who is the other? Who survived the battle apart from us and the accursed Asvatthama?'

'There is one who didn't fight the battle, but kept his peace.'

'Who is that?'

'Maya.'

'The architect?'

'Yes, him. Remember, Duryodhana made him a king when he built the palace for him after yours. He is still alive as he did not fight on either side of the war. You have not yet defeated him, so he is still a king.'

The King gasped in amazement. How did Krishna know everything! But where was this royal architect?

'As it happens, at present, he is living where your young maiden comes from. Indeed, I can see right now that he is beginning to feel the same disquiet about your guest as you are.'

'My lord, you are all and you know all.'

'Let me take the maiden back to her house. She knows Maya

and he will be the right person to help her cross the big divide between maidenhood and womanhood.'

The King was at once bewildered and relieved by Krishna's knowledge. Somehow Krishna had stitched all threads of information in his head. He fell at Krishna's feet, but was raised immediately by the Dark One.

Back in the King's bedroom, the poor girl lay still, comatose. Krishna picked up the maiden as if she were but a doll and took her outside. The chariot was still there. Krishna got into it, still holding the girl in his arms. The woman charioteer looked surprised, but nodded when he told her where he wanted to go.

∾

Every inch of Maya's body was taut. The woman beside him was now fast asleep, sated as she had not been for many days. But he was awake. He realized he had misgivings about the girl who had gone for her appointed night at the palace. As soon as he heard the rumble of the chariot, he got up and dressed. The woman stirred too, but wouldn't have woken up had Maya not nudged her gently.

'I think they have brought her home.'

'But it is still dark outside. Why is she back already?'

'You'd better go look.'

Dressing hastily, the woman got up and went to the door. She nearly fainted when she saw Lord Krishna at her doorstep. In his arms was her daughter. In her confusion, she forgot to bow to Krishna and immediately stretched her arms to take her child.

'Is she dead?'

'No, just asleep. Let me come in.'

The woman stepped aside, casting a hasty glance behind her to see if Maya had followed her.

'There is no need to hide Raja Maya; I know you are here. It is you I wish to talk to.'

Once Krishna called him, Maya knew that it was useless to pretend or explain. Acceding to his request, Maya came out and greeted Krishna. They had not seen each other since those days in Indraprastha. Neither had aged much. As always, Krishna had his ways of finding out about everything. The wily devil!

'What can I do for you, my lord?'

'You have to help me, help the King and rescue this kingdom from a terrible curse, which would descend on it if this young maiden was to see the sunrise without the feel of a man inside her. The King has lost his capacity tonight to perform his royal duty. You are royal yourself, I know. There is none beside you.'

'But why should there be a curse on the kingdom?'

'Don't you see? It is a king's dharma to perform royal duties. If he fails, the consequences befall the kingdom. It's the king's duty to deflower virgins if there is no prospect of finding a husband. The war has taken away all the young men and even the older ones. In that case, the king must perform his dharma, his raja dharma. That is our duty.'

'But if the king fails to do his duty, why does the kingdom suffer and not the king?'

'The king embodies the welfare of the kingdom. If the king falters, the kingdom suffers. When the kingdom suffers, the king grieves.'

'But is the kingdom not suffering already?'

'Yes.'

'Was the war just then? Was it the king's dharma to fight the war and kill all these people?'

'It was the adharma of Duryodhana that caused the war. It was the king's duty to fight and restore dharma.'

'But in the process, did he not cause many deaths?'

'You face the same problem, Raja Maya, as Arjuna did. You believe that wars are the result of an individual's actions. I had to explain to Arjuna on the eve of the battle that the war was caused by a cosmic disturbance. Whenever dharma is in disgrace,

I have to advise whosoever the suitable instrument at hand there is to restore it.'

'But you did not fight yourself, my lord.'

'No, it was not necessary for me to do so. There were the Pandava princes at hand. They had been wronged and they had to reclaim their right.'

'So was it Duryodhana that caused the suffering?'

'In a way, yes.'

'Why then is the King distressed by all the killings? It is not his fault; it is Duryodhana's.'

'It is not Duryodhana's fault in particular. After all, I could have been on his side if he had so chosen. I asked both Arjuna and him to tell me what they wanted from me. While Duryodhana chose my army, Arjuna chose me.'

'Did they choose or did you make them choose?'

'What do you mean?'

'Was it not your design that Duryodhana should choose badly?'

'Perhaps.'

'Did you not say that you had to restore dharma back to its true glory?'

'Yes.'

'Did you then cause all the killing and suffering by letting the war go ahead?'

'I don't think so about the killing. It was necessary to restore dharma.'

'But if it was necessary to kill all youth to restore dharma, why do you worry about a young maiden remaining unfulfilled?'

'It isn't her fate that worries me so much as the failure of the King to perform his duty.'

'But he failed because he thinks he was individually responsible for the suffering and killing.'

'I have told you he is not responsible. He didn't do anything out of his free will. It had to be done to restore dharma.'

'So what happened tonight is surely not his free will either?'

'No. This is his duty as a king. It is a king's dharma.'

'But what is this dharma which says the killing of all men in the kingdom is neither the King's fault, nor Duryodhana's? And now one young maiden remaining unfulfilled on one night becomes a matter of the king's responsibility.'

'You are being very obtuse, Raja Maya. Let me explain to you once again. It is not Yudhishthira who does or does not do something. A king has to perform a king's duties. When a king fails to carry out royal duties, it leads to nothing but a breakdown of dharma. It is then time for another king to restore dharma by performing that royal duty.'

'Even when the young maiden is not living in his kingdom and is not his subject?'

'When you have her, she is part of you, part of your kingdom. It is your kingship; when you are performing your king's dharma, she becomes your subject.'

'But my dear Dark Lord, in my kingdom it is not the king's dharma to deflower a virgin.'

'What do you mean?'

'If she were really in my kingdom, which is many days and many nights away, we would not think it to be the right of a king to have engaged in a war killing his cousins and uncles, losing all his soldiers and the youth of his own kingdom and many kingdoms. It would not be necessary for the king to deflower a virgin unless he was enamoured of her and she liked him. If there's no natural love, why engage in a meaningless physical activity?'

'You astonish me, Maya. You have always done so ever since I set eyes on you in the burning fires of Khandava. Pleasure has nothing to do with duty. A king performs his dharma because it is his duty to do so. He needn't get any pleasure from doing his duty.'

'But is that not precisely why he can't do his duty? You have converted the sensual act of a man and a woman being together into a duty.'

'He ought to get pleasure from consorting with his wife, but not with others.'

'In that case, what is the point of consorting with the others?'

'It is his duty!'

'But why is his duty not his pleasure?'

'If duty was to have pleasure, it would not be duty anymore.'

'My lord, now you are talking like one of them.'

'What do you mean?'

'You know what I mean. You are talking like those tall blond men, they who have killed and destroyed what they choose to call Aryavarta. You are not one of them, my lord. You, like me, are the dark one. We are not tall, nor blond, nor blue-eyed. We did not come from the land beyond the mountains in the north like they did. They came with their cattle and their hymns and settled here fighting all who lived here and then fighting within themselves. You are the dark one, as I am. You are neither a Kaurava, nor a Pandava. You tell me that Draupadi is your sister. I can quite believe this, since like you she is dark, but Subhadra your other sister, is fair, as is your brother Balarama.'

Raja Maya continued, 'As far as I can see, these tall people only know how to destroy. They will, everywhere they go. That is not so much a problem for me since they have kept me alive and given me a lot of their wealth. I do, however, mind that when they kill, they tell me they do it because it is their duty. When I kill, I do it because my survival depends on it. When I go hunting, I kill because I enjoy it. Either way, I kill because I want to. These tall men kill and they tell me they do so because it is their duty to do so. That I cannot understand.'

'But if killing is a pleasure for you, Maya, why do you ever stop?'

'Because nothing is a pleasure forever. I get tired of the sport, or my enemy is no longer there and the immediate danger is past. It is another day and life has moved on.'

'You may stop, but another may not. How do you make them stop?'

Maya had been brought up to respect craft, craftsmen and all those who worked with their hands. For him, Sudev was like a brother, one who had welcomed him into his house while they were building the palace.

When the construction of the palace was finished, Maya had gone out to look for the big buildings his father had told him about. He had gone out towards the Yamuna and the Ganga. He had sailed down, stopping wherever he saw some settlement. He had been wandering for many years, but had failed to find what he was looking for. Neither in Magadha, nor in the further east did he find the big structures he was looking for. By the time he had come back, Sudev was dead. Raghi was left to look after her daughter, with no help. Maya was allowed in her home. He did not tell anyone he had returned. The atmosphere between the two groups of cousins, who he had built the palaces for, had become quite poisonous. He had known a war was inevitable. He had kept his head down and settled in with Raghi.

Now, he had to find someone for Anuja and take care of Raghi.

⌐

Krishna was now back on his boat. Even while he was lying down, he could not stop thinking of Maya. Who was he? Where had he come from?

ॐ

13

Quetl I

Plop! Quetl woke up. A fish had jumped into his boat. He was surprised. He must have fallen asleep, perhaps fainted. He was famished. He had not had anything to eat for days. The sun was as hot as ever. In the middle of the water stretching all around him into the far distance, he felt stranded. He grabbed the fish that had jumped aboard, killed it and began to eat. He was hungry. He was also thirsty. The fish was salty and wet. He did not care. He crunched up the bones and the flesh quickly. It was as if he were worried it may disappear or jump back into the sea. He cupped some water in his hands and splashed on his face. The water was cool despite the heat of the day.

How long had he been at sea? He had lost track of time. How many cycles of the moon had he been sailing for? He recalled that when he began his journey, it had been raining heavily.

His father had been building the temple of the Great Serpent God. The King had wanted it ready for his coronation. Father was a master builder, he had built many temples—tall and broad, some rising from the ground, others built on top of a base of wooden frame. He was happy to take up the new challenge of building the temple, for which land had to be cleared. Then he drew the plan on the ground. To Quetl, he explained in great detail what he was doing. He did that for every building he constructed.

Quetl was going to be the master builder after him. The King would be happy to grant him that much. He had, after all, built for the king's father. He was the royal architect.

They were working hard and fast to finish the temple—he, his father and hundreds of helpers. Everyone wanted to assist in building the temple, which was only permissible following strict directions of his father. They were in a hurry. The temple had to be ready ahead of the coronation. It was almost done. But then the rains came early that year. Before they could finish, the skies opened up. There was a downpour of torrential rain, lashing the land day and night. They took shelter in a cave nearby, waiting for it to stop.

They hoped in vain. The rains would stay for three moon cycles—they knew that. This year, in fact, it went on to rain for two more moons. It was a bad omen, and the king was not pleased when told about it. He had to delay the coronation till the rain stopped. They returned to their cave, and another week went by. Quetl was sent out by his father to see how things were. After he reached the site, he was shocked. All the walls they had built lay collapsed. The stones were now lying in a heap, on top of one another. The temple, which had been built on earth and sand, had been washed away by the rain.

He ran back to his father and told him of the catastrophe. His father knew that that was the end—the king would sentence him to death. Though there was no escape for him, he wanted Quetl to live. He wanted him to become an even better builder than he was, and thus asked him to leave the land.

But where would Quetl go? The king's land stretched all around them. He would be caught. Even if he went to another kingdom, he would be caught and handed over.

'Go to the sea. Get a boat and sail away.'

'But where do I go?'

'Go in the direction in which the sun sets. Far away, there is the land where there are great builders. There are large plazas, temples and public baths. There are hundreds of people living together in that kingdom.'

'Where is it?'

'I don't know. I have heard that the sun in the sky is the same as here. It is hot there. You will have to go by the stars. Look out for the seven stars. They will guide you. You will have them above you when you get near the land.'

'I have never been at sea.'

'Don't argue. Go if you want to live. I want you to return and build the biggest temple anyone has seen. The people there will teach you. You must learn how to build temples that do not collapse just because it rains for a few days. Go now. Take my rings and bracelets. Get yourself a boat from someone.'

He had run day and night, and was at sea for ten days. He had no idea where he was going, except in the direction where the sun set. Sailors laughed at him. How will he reach his destination if he did not know where he was heading?

He did not know. But he did manage to buy a boat from them. The sailors showed him how to rig the sail and how to paddle. He was a stranger to all of this, and they knew he would not get very far on his own. They took pity on him, and gave him a sack of corn and avocados. Handing over a pot of water, they asked him to drink the water sparingly—that may last him a couple of months. If he survived, perhaps, they would find him drifting back.

Soon, he sailed off. It took him a while to learn how to even balance himself in the boat. It was still raining sparingly. But then the winds came from behind, off he went, speeding. The boat was small but steady. Occasionally, a wave came and drenched him. But soon he began to get the hang of sailing. He had to let the wind and the waves do the work for him. He had no control and little knowledge of where he was going. However, he did know that he had been sailing for a fortnight and his direction of travel had not changed.

Out at sea, he was collecting rainwater and drinking it. He ran out of the pot water even before the food was finished. He tried to scoop up sea water, but it was too salty. Land was nowhere to be seen. He sailed on. There were days when he was left battling hunger and thirst. He did not remember how long ago those days were. He must have fallen asleep or fainted. He had no idea.

The fish brought him to his senses, somehow. Having fed himself now, his brain started working. He could now think about where he was. The sea was calm. The wind seemed to have died down. His boat was drifting. He noticed its shadow on the water. Looking up at the sun, he could see that it had moved from above him, where it had been when he had set sail. It was now to his right, casting a shadow. He realized he had been away now for longer than five moons. There was no way of knowing what had happened to his father.

He looked around. No land could be seen on the horizon. But he noticed that the fish were more visible than before. Maybe he was getting better at noticing them. He thought he should try and catch one. Sitting down in his boat, he dipped his hand to see if he could catch one. He almost did. He stretched out further, but it looked like the boat would turn over. The boat had to be balanced and for that, he had to distribute his weight carefully. He was enjoying this new game.

The fish were enticing, but not easy to catch. He was determined to catch one, however. He managed to catch one, but it slipped away. He was so absorbed in his pursuit of catching a fish that he did not notice the boat coming towards him, one that was much bigger than his. Its sail was well rigged. The people on it began to shout and wave their arms. He was happy to see some human faces. But he was also afraid of what they would be like.

They came to the side of his boat, and a big man pulled him up. One of the men on the boat came down in his boat and started paddling the boat following the bigger one. Quetl was surrounded by about ten men. They were paler and had black hair, while his was red. Their eyes seemed narrower and closer together. Their upper body was bare, with a mere strip of cloth covering their nether parts. The big man who had pulled him up was clearly their leader. Quetl was not able to understand what the man was trying to tell him. Similarly, they could not grasp the language he spoke. So he opened his arms and moved forward to embrace the big man, who was not sure what the gesture meant. He took Quetl's hand and held it. That seemed like a gesture of friendship. The big man seemed to ask where Quetl had come from, to which he pointed towards the direction from where he had sailed. None was wiser.

Quetl was happy. He was, at last, no longer on his own. Whoever these people were, they might know where the land of the big buildings was. They may even be the people themselves. He will have to learn their language and explain what he was looking for. The big man patted his own stomach and then pointed to Quetl. In return, Quetl patted his stomach and pointed to his mouth. The big man laughed and called out to his men. They brought out a strip of dry meat. He had not eaten meat for so long. They laughed at how fast he ate. The big man signaled for more—Quetl had food and water to his heart's content.

They reached back to where the big boat had come from. In the harbour, there were many large boats, just like the one he had been hauled into. The land seemed big, but surrounded with water on all sides. Some women, along with children, were waiting on the quay to receive the boat. Their upper body, too, was bare like their men. They, however, wore a longer piece of cloth around their lower body. There was a big fish haul; the women moved swiftly and put the fish in baskets, which they carried on their heads. They were smaller than the men, but fairer. Their eyes were narrow, but somehow seemed more attractive to Quetl. He had not seen a woman for a very long time. Even back home, he had been busy working with his father.

There was a lot of curiosity surrounding him. Women were asking their men who had brought him, for which they had no response. He kept smiling. Not only was he a couple of hands taller than them but also stronger. Maybe with his red hair, he looked dangerous. The men from other boats came to look at him. They talked to the big man. There seemed to be a debate about what to do with him. The big man gestured and Quetl followed him. Other men were also coming along.

They had walked about a thousand steps when they came to a collection of three or four large huts. Each had a thatched roof made of coconut leaves. Each was made of mud and straw. Quetl's expert eyes told him that while the huts were large, they were not built on more than one level. The big man shouted something and bent down. The others did the same. Soon, a man came out of one of the huts. He was fatter than the rest and wore a necklace of what seemed to be animal bones. He was carrying a stick with a knob in his right hand, and was obviously their king.

The big man bowed, touching the ground, and said something in a loud voice. He brought Quetl forward. The king came closer to look at Quetl. He walked around him, appraising him. Quetl decided he must do what the others had done. He too bowed, touching the ground. The King drew a circle on the ground with his stick. Then he gave the stick to Quetl, who guessed that he was being asked where he had come from. The shape on the ground seemed to be a mark of where he was right now—the King's domain. Quetl drew a larger circle to the right of where the King had left the shape, signifying that he had come from a larger country, which was far away. He, consciously, left some distance between the two circles.

To Quetl's surprise, the King asked, 'Maya?' Quetl simply nodded his head. He had no idea how the King knew. Maybe he had sailed as far as his homeland. All the other men exclaimed aloud. They were expressing their wonder about how the King knew where this strange red-haired man had come from. The King was not done yet. He pointed to his hut and then upwards to the sky. Quetl understood what the King was saying—he wanted a big statue of himself and wanted more floors to be built in his hut.

Quetl was astounded. The King knew one thing about Maya— there they had big statues and big buildings. The word must have travelled among sailors from one boat to another. The King was probably a master sailor and had travelled much, visiting islands and continents.

From then on, Quetl understood that he had to build statues. He also had to make the King's large hut multistoried. This would not be easy. He would have to find stone, rocks and earth. Did this land have such things? He had to learn their language and find out more about what they had.

The King said something in a loud voice, hearing which a woman came out. She wore no clothes to cover her upper body like the rest of the women folk, but she had more necklaces laden on her than anyone else. Following her, two young girls came out. They must be the daughters. Quetl could not stop noticing their fine form. They did not seem concerned that he was staring at them; they were more curious about him. They quickly came forward to touch him and feel his strong arms. They laughed while admiring his red hair.

His first task was to look for materials that he needed to start building. He decided he would show his skills at building houses before starting work on the statue. There were men willing to help him. Wherever he went, young women also began to follow. They seemed to him very bold in the way they looked at him. And none seemed to mind their behaviour.

Walking around the place, he realized that it was an island. In his search for building materials, he was taken in boats to other nearby islands. By now, he knew it was a collection of islands. The people living on the other islands were similar to those he saw on his visit to the first one. The king seemed to be a powerful man, for he ruled some other islands too.

೧೧

14

Quetl II

Using sign language and gestures, Quetl succeeded in conveying to the king what was needed. He learned that the King was called Xa'tum. The King was quick to grasp Quetl's sign language. He took Quetl around the island to see what he could find. There were trees, especially those of coconut, which could provide some wood. However, there were not many options. He could not find stones or rocks; there was sand and clay, but not enough.

He noticed that the islanders used a lot of clay; they had clever designs and motifs for pots, beakers and plates made of clay. Almost every household followed some special way of shaping clay. Quetl was intrigued as to how they could use so much clay.

He started getting his answers when King Xa'tum took him for a ride to the nearby islands on his big boat, which was almost like a ship. Soon, Quetl understood that his island (as he had begun to think about it) was trading with other islands. The King hoped to sell his island's clay items and pigs.

Each island they visited welcomed them. Pigs were in maximum demand by one island that made baskets woven from coir. He noticed the way the islanders had ingeniously fashioned the bits and pieces torn from coconuts by stretching and binding them. Xa'tum sold some pigs and a lot of clay pots, and picked up many coir baskets. Quetl was puzzled; he had no use for coir baskets. He, soon, saw the reason: when they stopped at the next island, they exchanged the coir baskets for stone slabs. On another island, King Xa'tum dropped off some stone slabs and picked up timber. Quetl now understood that if he needed something, he could trade with other islands, either directly or through a parallel deal with two islands. There were a lot of islands nearby and they were trading constantly with one another.

Soon, he settled in a hut provided by the king. There was a large piece of clear land and Quetl had to get on with building. He asked Ra'pu, the big man who had brought him, to provide him with helpers. One of them was Ra'pu's son, Ra'nu. Quetl knew that the father wanted the boy to learn how to build from him, so he was given the task of explaining whatever Quetl wanted to be done by the helpers.

The island had ample food—pigs, rice and coconuts. And fish, prawns and crabs, of course. Quetl began to enjoy himself. He was the object of the islanders' curiosity. The women, who were attracted to his body, did not hesitate from coming into his hut to spend the night. They were fascinated by his red hair. He was taller and bigger than the other men on the island. This was what they liked. They were very good at letting him explore as he wanted. The older women were much bolder, while the younger ones were shy but eager. They had smooth skins and smelled of fish. He had begun to learn a few words and understand some more.

It had been a while since Quetl had been with a woman. His cousins were his playmates in childhood and gradually their games had become more intimate. But they were shy and took a lot of persuasion to unwind and indulge for the sake of pleasure. Here the younger women took to Quetl as their exotic plaything. They had had lovers before. But he was able to give them what they had not experienced. He let them inside his hut one at a time, but sometimes young girls came in pairs egging each other on. They did not come back after a night. Quetl found that very curious. Lovemaking was intense while they were there, but then he never saw them again. Or maybe he did not recall them as time passed. There was not much scope for building a lasting relationship in any case. Quetl knew that he had to move on with his work as soon as he could.

There seemed to be no seasons on the island, except rainy. It rained for a longer period than it did back home, but not heavily. He kept on going across to other islands when he needed some material. They knew him, so they let him pick up whatever he wanted. Xa'tum would later go to the island and settle the dues by selling something from his island. The back and forth among the islands made him remember walking down the road in his town back home.

Soon, the house was ready. It had a ground floor with four rooms. Then there were stairs on the outside, which took you to the floor above. Here there were two large rooms. The roof had a timber frame and coconut leaves strung together to provide cover. Quetl had carved a large serpent on the front door. He worshipped the serpent. Xa'tum loved it and wanted everyone to see it.

A big feast was organized. People from the surrounding islands came. Xa'tum was full of himself. Kings bigger than his stature were coming to see what he had. The entire island was in a celebratory mood. All the women were wearing ornaments and had made themselves up to look beautiful. The men wore their necklaces and wrist clasps. The other islanders had their own distinct skirt wraps, except that they were all bare on the top half. There must have been more than five hundred people.

Xa'tum took each important guest to see his new house. It was like a miracle for his visitors. They had never seen a staircase. Quetl was concerned if the structure would stand the strain of so many people walking up and down his newly built stairs. But somehow the structure stood up, unlike his father's temple. He had done something all by himself. He would be a builder, perhaps a master builder, one of these days. He had also trained Ra'nu, who had proved to be a good learner.

Among the many kings who had gathered, Quetl could see the one who stood out. He was taller than the rest of them, but smaller than him. He also looked much more like his people back home, though he had black and not red hair. He was fully dressed in a long dress, which looked like a gown. His legs were covered in a piece of cloth which was wrapped around his waist. Xa'tum was bowing to him every now and then.

The stranger was talking to Xa'tum and soon pointed to Quetl, who thought he wanted a building constructed on his island. That indeed proved to be the case. The stranger king was called Rotolu, and he wanted Quetl to come to his island. Quetl agreed, as he saw his chance to move on from the island he had been living in. Xa'tum conveyed that Rotolu lived far away on a big island. That was even better for Quetl. He could not wait. But Xa'tum was reluctant. He began to argue with Rotolu about bringing Quetl back soon. Rotolu was adamant—he was a bigger king. Xa'tum agreed. Rotolu asked one of his servants to bring something—it was a jade necklace. He presented it to the queen. Everyone gasped in admiration. The deal was done. Quetl was traded for a jade necklace.

Fond farewells were said. Quetl realized how much he had come to like the islanders. They were simple and friendly. Women came and hugged him, reminding him of the many nights he had enjoyed with them. They were happy he had been there. They were obviously used to visitors moving on. After one last hug from Xa'tum, Quetl climbed on to Rotolu's large boat. They were a flotilla of ten boats. Quetl had no idea where he was headed. He hoped they would move further in the direction of the setting sun. In a short while, after some quick manoeuvres, the flotilla began to move in the direction Quetl had hoped for.

This was the second journey at high seas for Quetl. But unlike his first journey, now he was in the hands of skilled sailors. The flotilla had ample food and water. The principal boat even had a small hut on it, which helped them keep dry when it rained. Rotolu showed Quetl where he would sleep in the hut. Quetl had no idea how long their journey would be or even where they were headed. As before, he was relying on his sense of direction and his good luck to get him to his destination.

It was time for his lucky streak. Next day, Rotolu called a sailor from one of the other boats to come on to theirs. Quetl heard Rotolu talk to the sailor, and the only word he could recognize from their conversation was 'Maya'. To his surprise, the sailor spoke to him in his own language. He asked Quetl his name and where he came from. Quetl decided that there was no point in hiding anything. The sailor then asked him where he was headed. Happily, he told the man about the land where there were big buildings. The sailor seemed to recognize the description. He started conveying to Rotolu what he had learnt. Rotolu, nodding his head, indicated that it was in the same direction they were were headed, but farther away.

Later, when they were alone, Quetl asked the sailor how he knew his language. The sailor, whose name was Hopu, said he had been to Quetl's land in search of jade and other precious stones, accompanying Rotolu on his boat. But when Rotolu could not pay what the jade traders had asked for, he left five of his men as guarantee, while he went to obtain the money. Hopu and his friends had to work hard. They got food, but barely anything else. They, somehow, learnt the language, along with various other aspects about the people they had been left under the care of. Rotolu came after several months. He took them back after paying the dues for the jade.

Hopu was happy knowing he could use the knowledge he had so painfully acquired. Two of his fellow sailors had died while waiting for Rotolu to return, and, thus, Hopu counted himself lucky. Now, Rotolu would value him more as he could interpret what Quetl was trying to convey.

Quetl realized that without his only skill—of building—he, too, would have ended up being someone's slave like Hopu. He too would have been pledged for a debt and left to die if things changed for the worse and he could not be redeemed.

Having Hopu around meant that for the first time in many moons, Quetl was not lonely. He had never imagined that having someone you could talk to would be so important. Though Hopu knew only rudimentary bits of his language, with Quetl's help, he was able to expand his vocabulary. Quetl found that Hopu had been a sailor for most part of his life. His family had very little to eat and feed the many children they had. Hopu had been sold off to Rotolu when he was very young, and now could no longer remember how old he was or how many years he had been sailing for.

Quetl began to teach Hopu how to tell time and how to calculate days and nights as they passed. As they sat at night looking at the sky, Quetl helped Hopu learn to note how the moon waxed and waned. He taught Hopu how to count the days from one full moon to the next. He showed him how to make marks on a stick, which would help him keep a track of how many cycles had passed. Though Hopu faced some difficulty in understanding things, he kept on asking Quetl to explain those to him.

ೞೞ

15

Rotolu's Island

Rotolu's island was much bigger than Xa'tum'.

The people, however, were friendly just the same. The women were smoother skinned, dark and had sparkling eyes. They were bare above and wrapped a piece of cloth lower down. The men were similarly dressed, but taller than the ones he had seen on Xa'tum's island.

Quetl did not take much time to settle down. Bigger the island, the greater were his chances to find building materials. And, of course, there was Hopu. From the very first day, Rotolu had made it clear that he wanted Quetl to build a house similar to what he had built for Xa'tum. But it had to be bigger.

Hopu explained to Quetl that a big feast, organized by Rotolu, was nearing. Many kings from far away islands were to come. Rotolu was thrilled at the prospect of being able to show off the big house Quetl was building for him. And it was not just the house he was excited about. Rotolu had noticed the big painting of the serpent that Quetl had made for Xa'tum. He was keen on Quetl painting a gigantic version of the drawing for him too.

Quetl was asked to paint a serpent on a separate structure before he started building the palace. This time, he could have as much help as he wanted, with Hopu translating by his side. He had decided to build a tall wall, one that would not wash away in the rains. For this, mud and clay would not suffice. He had to find stone in large quantities. He asked Hopu to take him around the island to get an idea of what was available. Hopu knew that there were neighbouring islands from where they could get what was not available nearby.

Hopu took him along in a boat. They were just skirting the island along the edge. Quetl was puzzled when Hopu swerved the boat and went along a river, going upstream. The area around was devoid of any habitation. Hopu suddenly stopped, and jumped out asking Quetl to follow. Quetl was surprised to find himself at the foot of a hill. He had not expected to come across a hill of such a size there. Unlike Xa'tum's island, there were a lot of topographical variations on this one. Hopu began to walk uphill along a steep path, and Quetl tried to keep pace with him.

Hopu stopped at what looked like a resting place. It was a large cave. The ground was slightly levelled. He shouted something— it was obviously to call someone. He shouted again. From the darkness of the cave, a man walked out.

Quetl was taken aback at the sight before his eyes. In front of him stood a man, thin but tall. His head was smooth on top except for a tuft of hair around the edges, he had long matted hair, with a clean-shaven face. Indeed, there was more hair on the man than Quetl had ever seen before. But it was his eyes which captivated him—they were clear and dark black, with a shine. They sparkled with humour and mystery.

Hopu went down and fell at the man's feet. Quetl took the hint and did the same. Hopu began to explain to the man why he had brought Quetl to him. Quetl was not sure how the man could help, but then he had no option than to rely on Hopu.

The man came up to Quetl and looked at him intensely. He started muttering, walking around him and looking at him from every angle. Then he uttered something that Quetl did not understand. Hopu asked Quetl to show the man his hand. As he held out his arm, the man grasped it and studied the palm. He stared at the palm intensely for what seemed like an eternity. Then he started laughing and dancing. Not knowing what to do, Quetl simply stood there. Finally, the man stopped and fell silent.

Quetl looked at Hopu as if to ask what was going on, and he explained that the man was a man of God—which God, Hopu did not say. He told Hopu that Quetl was born to be great, and that he was not to stay on the island for long. He was going to be abducted by the devil, who would take him far away. The devil would be friendly. Wherever he ends up, Quetl would be the king of that land.

Quetl asked Hopu if he knew the name of that man. Hopu said, 'He is called Narada. He is a muni, a very holy man who travels everywhere, spreading knowledge and news.'

'How far away has he come from?'

'I am told it would take a full moon cycle to reach there by boat.'

Hopu asked the holy man another question. The man pointed to a cave, which was a few yards away. Hopu again fell at his feet. Quetl thought it best to do the same. They left the holy man after that.

As they walked away, Hopu explained that many holy men had come through recently. The islanders were being told they had to light a fire and offer sacrifices. They had to choose a god to worship. The holy men told them about different gods. The islanders were advised that they should worship the Serpent God, Naga. Many were sceptical, but Rotolu had been won over. He had welcomed these holy men who taught them all how to behave, what to eat and how to worship.

These holy men also knew how to build big monuments. Hopu had asked Narada where he would find suitable stone slabs for Quetl. The holy man had directed them towards the other cave.

ನಞ

16

Takshak I

'So how did you meet Takshak?' Krishna asked.

They had been gently drifting along the Saraswati. Anuja seemed to have calmed down and was sleeping in her mother's arms. Krishna was still thinking of Radha and the brief reunion they had had. He cursed himself and all the people who had come to him for help. He had looked after everyone but himself. Perhaps that was the way for a yogi.

He had been helpless when asked by Radha about her son. Where would he be on the vast land of Kurukshetra? He decided to probe this mysterious man who had dragged him away from the battlefield to return to Dwarka.

'It is a long story. But I met him on an island—it would take a full moon cycle to reach there from here by boat. I had reached that island after many moon cycles, going from island to island and being handed over from one king to another. They all wanted me to build them houses made of stone. Then, the King asked me to build a big statue of a serpent. I had no idea why I was being asked to do so, but I was familiar with these figures and had learned to paint them from my father.'

'They never had anyone build them as big a serpent stone as I did. The King held a consecration ceremony and invited other kings from all around. But Takshak was the biggest king of all.

They all bowed down to him. He saw the serpent monument and asked who the sculptor was. So I was presented to him. That was it. He just took me away with him after I was passed on to him from King Rotolu, who in turn had bought me from another. I got on his big ship, and now here I am.'

'Did he ask you to build a palace for him? Is that what you were doing when we found you in the middle of the Khandava forest?'

Maya continued, 'He brought me back and we sailed all the way up the Ganga and then the Yamuna. He seemed to be in a big hurry, but even then we had to stop as his people had come to meet him and pay their tributes. They told him the stories of their lives. They all seemed to be about fighting the Aryas who were chasing them away from their lands.'

'Takshak told me that there was a time when the entire country, west of Magadha, belonged to his people. They occupied lands, forests and also built houses. They even had forts. But the Aryas, who had come with their horses, chariots and sharp arrows, began to clear them away. The Nagas were no match for them. They had to find different ways of fighting the Aryas or they would be decimated.'

'So he brought you to build better forts?'

'Forts and palaces with barricades. He wanted to know what weapons we used in my country. I taught him about plants and poisons. His idea was to create another empire of the Nagas where there was once before.'

'That is why you were hard at work even in the forest?'

He nodded, saying, 'Till you ruined my plans of building a palace for him in the Khandav forest. Takshak was furious. He has not yet forgiven you. He says he will take revenge on the entire Kuru clan. He wants to end the line.'

'The Kurus have done a very good job of ending the line themselves. Who is left? The Pandavas? Even they are hardly from the original Kuru line. Pandu was a Kuru, but these are not his children. Nor were Duryodhana and his brothers the natural sons of their father. Bhishma was the last who could have kept the line going by having his own children, but then that clever woman Satyavati said the throne had to go to her children and only her children.'

'But they are all progeny of Vyasa, aren't they? So, it is her line if not her husband Shantanu's.'

'Vyasa Dwaipayana is above these mundane matters. What he will leave behind is eternal.'

'Takshak is still angry. He told me that no matter how many Aryas are killed, he would not give up his plan for revenge. I don't know what he plans to do but his people are now scattered all over Aryavarta, hiding and waiting to strike and kill.'

Krishna did not say anything. His mind immediately turned to Uttara. He concentrated for a while to ascertain if Uttara was alright. He did not like what his mind's eye saw.

ನಲ

17

Draupadi's Moment

Draupadi had been lying awake for hours. The rule that she was to be accompanied by one of her husbands every night was followed through all these years. But the rule provided that the nights she was bleeding were her own. It had been three days since the day she was supposed to bleed. She could not believe it. Was it a curse by that insane Brahmin, Asvatthama? But she was sure that if anything was to happen, Krishna would take care of her.

Could it be that her dearest wish had been fulfilled by Arjuna? Was she going to bear his child? Was it that early morning of the first day of the war when Arjuna had come back to her and had been so masterly that the deed was done? Draupadi thought and began to count the days backward. Yes. That must have been the night or the very early hours of the morning. She had only seen him once after the war, when he was so depressed, but she had cheered him up.

Yes. That early morning of the first day of the war had to be the day. Will she leave behind a Kuru prince from the original line, unlike Uttara, who was carrying the grandson of that cowherd Subhadra? What could she do? Who should she tell? Krishna had gone off to Dwarka. If she were to have a son, as she had five times already, then her son should become the next king. Uttara's child had no right. Whom could she go to to settle the matter?

She lived in the huge palace with her five husbands, but had not told them about her state. They did not need to know, and she liked the nights when she could rest. They would not understand anyway. Now that the war was over, she felt she had to free herself from her earlier life. She had done her duty, sacrificed many years and lost her five dear sons for the sake of dharma. Now her dharma was different. Her dharma now was to win the throne for Arjuna and herself. But who could she see to discuss the conundrum?

She thought of the others. There was the old blind king Dhritarashtra and his queen Gandhari. They had withdrawn from life, but lived on despite their desire to follow their sons. There was Kunti, whom Draupadi never forgave for her order, following which she had to be shared by all five brothers, while it was Arjuna alone who had won the contest and captured her heart. There was Vidura, but he, too, would ask her to follow dharma. She needed someone who was above all these elders.

She tossed and turned. Why was Krishna not here? Could she pray to him? He always heard her prayers no matter however far he was. Then it suddenly dawned on her. It was Vyasa, the grand sire of all, who she could consider. He was the progenitor of the saga, the great Muni. She had to ask him for help. He would grant her the wish she had. She had never asked him before for anything. Her child would be from his line, but Uttara's would be from an inferior queen's son.

ನ೮

18

The Elders

They always sat in the part of the palace where the sun shone till the longest time. They wrapped themselves up every morning and came to this favourite place of theirs. It was as if that Maya Danav had thought about their old age and provided a corner blessed by the sun.

Gandhari was silent as usual and blindfolded. Dhritarashtra sat near her. They never said a word to each other, not since the war had ended and all their sons had perished. If anyone talked, it was Vidura. He was still trying to figure out what he could have done to stop the massacre. The only person who was willing to listen was Kunti. Of all the members of the Kuru family, she had survived with the least hurt. Her sons had won. Though she had lost her five grandsons, Uttara gave her hope.

Vidura was worried about Uttara. Like Bhishma, his desire to live had a limit. Thus, he needed to ascertain whether the Kuru line would continue. He felt responsible towards them. Of the three sons of Vyasa Dwaipayana, he was the only one who could have given children. He was still alive, with Pandu dead a long time ago, and Dhritarashtra as good as dead.

He asked Kunti, 'Have you seen how Uttara is?'

'Why? Are you worried?'

'I had a disturbing dream last night. A serpent was gnawing at Uttara's womb. I could not kill the serpent.'

'Let us go see her.'

Kunti knew that he would worry the whole day unless she put his mind at rest. Worrying about everyone else seemed to be his life's mission these days.

So they stood up very slowly, with the help of women attendants in the palace. Vidura took more time to get up. Kunti was still able to move about. She was the youngest among them.

She shivered a little as they went indoors. The palace was big and it was a long walk before they reached the section where Uttara was confined. She was awake, but seemed to be breathing heavily. Vidura's dream was prescient. She was throwing up. She looked haggard. There was a *vaid* sent from her father's palace to look after her. He was one of the few men who was left alive, as he had not gone to Kurukshetra.

Vidura asked Karuna, the vaid, 'How is she?'

'She slept very badly. I gave her a drink mixed with herbs and she quietened down. But she has had a restless night. If she does not recover soon, I fear she might lose the baby.'

'These are still early weeks. Her body has to get used to the change,' Kunti said relying on her vast experience.

'Still, after ten weeks, she should be heavier than she is,' Karuna said.

'Who knows how many weeks? It has only been a month since Abhimanyu fell.'

'We do not know when he planted the seed,' Kunti said.

Vidura was now convinced that his dream was nothing short of a warning.

'Is there any way of finding out how big she should be? Can we call another vaid?'

'Where are you going to find another vaid?' Kunti said. She knew how many people had died—they were not just soldiers, but all the helpers too.

Vidura was not willing to give up.

'Maybe there are women in Hastinapur who could help. Let us ask.'

The women attendants talked among themselves. Then one said, 'There is one old woman. I have not seen her for many years, but she may be able to help. I could go into the city and ask for her.'

Vidura wanted someone to take immediate action to salve his worried mind.

'Yes. Go and find the woman and bring her here.'

Uttara moaned. She was trying not to throw up. She wanted to rest. She opened an eye and saw Kunti and Vidura. She thought it best to go on pretending to be asleep. It was going to be difficult, but she must try till they went away.

The elders asked so many questions of her. To her, they were strangers. She had not seen Vidura before and had only seen Kunti on the day she got married. She felt she did not belong there. They only cared about the child she was carrying. She thought of Abhimanyu again and stayed within herself.

After sobbing, she sat up. She was starting to feel sick again. The women got to work, bringing another silver bowl for her to throw up in. She cried out in pain. The women patted her and gave her cold water to clean her mouth. She was still gasping for breath and could not stop vomiting.

Vidura, turning to the woman who knew the old lady who could help, said, 'Run quickly. Take a chariot if you need one, but find the woman and bring her here.'

Vidura said to Kunti, 'We need to talk about this. Come.'

Uttara was relieved that they had gone. She never felt comfortable when the elders were around. She lay down again. One of her attendants began to fan her. She quickly fell asleep, dreaming about Abhimanyu and her baby.

19

Vyasa

The news of Uttara's convulsions spread rapidly among the women attendants. News that someone had been sent to find an old woman acquired a life of its own. Someone said she must be a powerful witch to rescue Uttara's child. Others said they knew that woman, but she had died a while ago. Had Uttara already lost her child? Rumours swirled around.

When Draupadi heard those rumours, she was sure Krishna had heard her wish and caused this sickness. She had to move fast. She had to see Dwaipayana Vyasa.

She had heard that Vyasa was in the palace recording the events of the war. There was a rumour that Ganesha was helping him in this task. Draupadi knew she would not be able to see Ganesha as he would stay invisible, but Vyasa was human and thus could be helpful.

She had to find out where he was in the Hastinapur Palace. This was not their palace, but Duryodhana's. She maybe the queen now, but still felt like an outsider. She decided to ask the one person she trusted.

Vidura was still worried about what had happened earlier in the day. He had gone back with Kunti to sit with the others. But then as the sun moved, they had returned to their rooms. Vidura had tried to make Kunti understand the gravity of the situation, but she was now beyond all that. She was philosophical about the future of the Kuru lineage. The Kurus had been horrible to her husband and even more so to her sons. She had got her revenge. She did not care anymore.

When Draupadi entered, Vidura was reflecting on the Kuru lineage with his eyes shut. It took him some time to notice Draupadi standing with folded hands. As he opened his eyes, Draupadi fell at his feet.

'What brings you here, O Queen?'

'I hear that Mahamuni Vyasa is in the palace. I would like to see him.'

'I can take you to him. But why do you want to see him?'

Draupadi had anticipated the question and was prepared with the answer.

'Uncle, I hear that the Mahamuni is writing an account of the war. I want to tell him about the bravery of my brother Dhrishtadhyumna.'

'Do you think he does not know already?'

'I realize he knows everything. But a sister's heart wants to make sure that her brother gets the justice he deserves.'

'I thought you may want to tell him about Arjuna.'

'No. I am sure that Arjuna will get his due in any story of the war.'

By this time, Vidura had led Draupadi to the part of the palace where Vyasa had his seat. Vidura knocked on the door. A voice from within said, 'Come Vidura.'

Ganesha, who was sitting with him, ready with his pen, disappeared, as he did anytime someone came to see Vyasa.

Vyasa saw Draupadi with Vidura and smiled. He had not seen the dark beauty for many years. He could see why that face and that figure had caused such destruction.

Draupadi bowed down fully in pranam, paying obeisance to Vyasa. Vidura left silently.

'Drupad's daughter, what brings you here?'

'Grandfather of all, nothing is hidden from you. I have come with a wish which you alone can grant me.'

'I can guess. For a woman who has suffered as much as you have—losing your husbands' kingdom, going into exile, wandering in forests, then losing your five fine sons—your misery has been endless. I can guess what your wish is, but do tell me yourself.'

'Grandfather, you know there is only Uttara left to give birth to a prince to keep your line alive. That is what everyone says. But these are early days and I hear that she may lose her child. I have come to ask you to bless the child I believe I am carrying. I have not told anyone, not even Arjuna, whose child it is. I want you to protect my womb and my child so that he can be the next ruler.'

'My beautiful and indeed dutiful daughter, I have known for some time about your eagerness to assuage the hurt caused by the loss of your princes. Everyone knows that you have ever only loved Arjuna. You have done your duty to your other four husbands, but that was a *tapasya*.'

'Grandfather, please grant me my wish. I have never asked anything else of you.'

'You have no need of anyone. You have Krishna.'

'I have not prayed to him. This is a matter of your family. You are the grandfather who made it all possible.'

Vyasa remained silent. He went into a state of *samadhi* for what seemed like an eternity to Draupadi. She knew she had to stay silent. Vyasa finally opened his eyes. He sighed as he smiled.

'I have been communing with Bhagwan Krishna. You are asking me to change the order of the world. I can help you, but I need to ask Krishna, as he is the guardian of the order of the world.'

Draupadi was stunned. This was a world of men above all the men and women, dead or alive. She did not know what to expect. She had to be patient.

'Granddaughter, I can see that Uttara is going to lose her

child in a short while. Your womb has got the prince who will survive. But there is one harsh condition.'

'What is it, Grandfather?'

'It will be your child, but we have to plant it in Uttara's womb.'

A stunned Draupadi broke out in sobs.

'Why Grandfather?'

'That is the order of the world. You lost your sons, but have your husbands, especially Arjuna. Uttara has lost her father and her husband. She has nothing but her foetus. If she loses that too, there will be no one more unfortunate than her.'

'You are asking me once more to give up a precious possession. Do I only do my duty and never get my reward?'

'The order of the world is not kind to individuals. It is designed to sustain all who are here now and will be in the future. Kunti told her sons to share you equally. You favour Arjuna, giving him two sons, while the others had only one. This violates your duty. Krishna says you cannot be seen flouting your duty. No one will know except you.'

'I go away empty handed once again. I have sustained the family, but go away with nothing.'

'No, Daughter. You alone will know that whoever becomes the successor to Yudhishthira will be your child and not Uttara's. Arjuna's child will succeed, not his grandchild. You are the creator. Uttara will merely carry your child. You will have saved my *kula*. I must salute you for that.'

Vyasa folded his hands and bowed deep.

Draupadi was in a daze. Had she won or lost? She and she alone, apart from the Mahamuni, will be party to the great secret. Tears flowed down her face. But she was smiling as she said to Vyasa, 'Bhagwan, you are the master of my fate and I bow to you.'

Vyasa said, 'Sit here for a while, as I transfer your child to Uttara's womb. No one will find out.'

Draupadi was crying and smiling and overwhelmed by the

power of Vyasa. She sat there, while he worked his miracle. She could feel her body changing. She was amazed.

Vyasa opened his eyes. He was smiling benignly. Draupadi fell at his feet again. He blessed her by putting his hands on her head. 'It is done. Your child will be the king!'

Draupadi knew it was time to go. As she walked away, she knew she was bleeding gently.

Ganesha appeared back on his seat, his pen at the ready. He just raised an eyebrow. Did he have to write down what he had heard?

Vyasa said, 'Write.'

Ganesha was ready.

'Asvatthama, in his hatred of the Pandavas, put a curse on Uttara to make her lose her child. But Krishna intervened. He thwarted Asvatthama's attack. Uttara's child was saved.'

Vyasa saw Ganesha wondering if he was serious. Vyasa said, 'I communed with Krishna and he ordered me to do what I did and also write what I told you.'

Ganesha knew that it was an order and he could not disobey. He began to write.

ೞ

20

Krishna

Krishna had been quiet for a while. Maya did not disturb him. He knew Krishna did more than just talk to him. His mind was always engaged in things which went on around the world. Maya never knew how Krishna could do so many things and what was the secret behind his powers. Everyone he had met acknowledged Krishna as the Master. Some even called him God. Maya never discovered the secrets of his power, but ever since the day Krishna and Arjuna had rescued him, he knew who was the Master.

Krishna was sad. He had never been so downhearted. He knew how Draupadi must have felt when she had to give up the child in her womb. He was surprised when Vyasa communed with him. The question proposed to him was a difficult one, but not the first of sorts. Draupadi was like a sister to him—she thought of herself as his sister. He had known her since the time she had emerged fully formed from the sacrificial fire when he had visited her father's kingdom in Panchala. He had seen her grow up with her brother Dhrishtadhyumna. She was a striking dark beauty, fiery in nature. Krishna had made up his mind that she would be married to Arjuna. Kunti's children needed some real royal backing. Drupada would provide that if his daughter was wed to Arjuna. Krishna had suggested the contest where princes were invited to participate in the archery competition; the winner was to win Draupadi's hand in marriage. He knew that only Arjuna had the skill to win the event.

What he had not anticipated was that Kunti would complicate his scheme. Once she asked the brothers to share the prize Arjuna had won, Krishna was bound by that decision. He could not undo it. This is why after all these years he had to deny Draupadi her rightful claim to have a child in her womb who could succeed Yudhishthira someday. Krishna could not undo Kunti's injunction. It was part of the order of things, of dharma. Draupadi could not consciously elevate one of her husbands above the others, not even Arjuna, not even after all that had happened on the fields of Kurukshetra. Dharma had to be upheld. So he had to tell Vyasa about the hard decision he had to convey to Draupadi. He knew she would be devastated. But in the larger scheme of things, this was a justice of sorts. She, at least, knew that it was her child who would continue the line. Only Vyasa and he were aware—between Vyasa and himself, they knew everything there was to know. But this morning, Krishna felt that the burden of knowing was unbearable. This followed the news of Radha's loss, and that made him sad.

Maya knew instinctively that Krishna was not his usual self. He left him alone. He had Anuja to worry about. She was still recovering from the shock of that horrible night. Maya was determined to protect her as long as he could. He knew that his time of departure from this land was nearing. He had not found what he had come for. Instead, he had become an object of curiosity himself. People wondered looking at his palaces, but he knew there were better buildings somewhere near. Takshak was going to take him there, but first he had to build him a palace. That palace for Takshak was never built, and the one that had been, unleashed events that nearly led to the annihilation of the Aryas. Maybe, Takshak is happy, he thought.

Krishna asked, as if he had read Maya's mind. 'Have you seen

Takshak recently? Do you know where he is?'

'You know these things better than most of us. I know that he wanted to be out of the way as he knew some conflict will break out when the Pandavas returned from their exile. He told me he wanted to see how his scattered troops were faring. He wants to gather them and attack what remains of the Aryas.'

'Tell him not to try. Yudhishthira is not to be underestimated. He will perform an Asvamedha yajna to establish his command over the Aryabhumi. Takshak should save his troops.'

'Why are you being so friendly with Takshak?'

'You may not know, but I have some Naga blood in me.'

'How can that be?'

'My father Vasudeva's father was Shura. He was Kunti's father as well. His mother was a Naga princess.'

'Tell me more.'

'The reason I left Mathura and took the Vrishnis to Dwarka is because we come from this part of the country. This was a prosperous land a few generations ago. Saraswati was a much bigger river and there were settlements around here. But then the rains started failing. Life became hard. My grandfather Shura was the leader of our people. They were cattle herders and lived by producing milk and butter, which other people exchanged with their produce. My grandfather had travelled extensively, so he knew that if he led his people away from here towards where there were big rivers, he was sure to find fertile land to settle. He took his extended family with him. He knew where there were better pastures. He, thus, led the people to Yamuna.'

Krishna went on, 'He contacted the local kings. He had many skills—in medicine, in fortune-reading. He knew many languages. He was liked by the local king. He asked for a large tract of land where he could settle his people. This is how the Vrishnis settled in Gokul. My father grew up around Gokul. He inherited a lot of the skills of his father and passed those on to me. He attracted the attention of kings around the Ganga–Yamuna

confluence. Kamsa was very fond of him and wanted him as his
advisor. His sister Devaki married my father.'

'I have heard that Kamsa put Devaki in prison.'

'It was a part of his palace where my father and mother were
confined. They had all the comforts, but Kamsa took away all
the children born to them. He did that because he was told that
Devaki would give birth to a son who would kill him.'

'You?'

'Yes.'

'Is that why the other kings like Sisupala and Jarasandha
hated you?'

'Yes. The other kings were harassing our people in Gokul, so
I decided to bring them back to where they had come from. I
brought them further south, looking for a land which received
proper rain. I knew the land around Dwarka that had ample
pastures. So I led them across from Yamuna to Saraswati and
then down to Dwarka.'

'That is one story about you I had never heard before.'

'No, they all believe I am one of them. When Shura came
to Gokul, not only my father, but his sister also came along.
Then King Kuntibhoj liked her so much, he asked if he could
adopt her. My grandfather knew he would need many friends in
the new place where he had brought his people. So he agreed.
Kunti was the name Kuntibhoj gave her. So Kunti became a part
of the Aryas. Kunti attracted Pandu's attention. Since my father
had also been seen in the company of kings, everyone thought
I must be from around here. They have made up some fantastic
tales about my family.'

'I am never sure how you will surprise me next.'

'You helped the King out of his difficulty and saved his
kingdom from ruin. You have fulfilled your mission. Let me show
you what Takshak has so far failed to show you. You came from
a land many moons ago to see some great buildings. You have
been searching for them for many years. Your search is now about

to end. Nearby are the buildings and cities you came to see.'

To Maya's astonishment, Krishna asked the sailors to stop the boats. He directed them to a spot where they could disembark. The chariot had been keeping pace on the land, moving along the river. Raghi and Anuja were helped down by Krishna. Maya came out last, not very sure what Krishna was about to do.

'Get into the chariot. We have not long to go. Our elephant will catch up with us. The sailors will guide it.'

As soon as they all got in, Krishna asked the woman handling the chariot to sit behind with the others and took over the task of driving the chariot. He seemed to know where he was going. They were going uphill. After a while, Maya began to see why Krishna had stopped here. The horizon began to display tall, deserted buildings made of clay bricks and stones.

Krishna was not stopping yet. He kept on going. Raghi and Anuja, too, were astonished at what they saw. Though the whole place was deserted, they could spot house after house. Krishna continued till he came to a large open space. It was surrounded by large buildings on all four sides.

They all got off. Maya immediately knew that this must be the site he had been told about. He was waiting for the next surprise.

Krishna looked around as if hoping to find someone. Then he called out, 'Takshak Raja, you can come out now. I have got him for you.'

To Maya's surprise, Takshak came out from a tall building on their right. Maya had not seen him for years, but he still looked the same. He was tall and slim with a sinewy body. As usual, he had a serpent draped around his neck but it was his pet serpent, which was quite friendly. He moved elegantly, almost sliding rather than walking. Takshak bowed down before Krishna. Krishna clasped his shoulders and embraced him. They were like long-lost friends.

'I told you I will find him and bring him to you one of these days,' Krishna said to Takshak.

'A whole bloody war intervened and thousands have died before you found him for me!'

'Don't complain. Those who died were never going to be your friends. But here is someone all the way from across the waters. He is now eager to get back to his homeland. Before leaving, he must see what he has come for. You are the best person to show him.'

Maya was speechless. He hugged Takshak and they held each other for a while. Krishna made the next move.

'Raja Maya, Takshak and you can happily spend the days going around from town to town. I will take Raghi and Anuja with me to Dwarka. Rukmini and Satyabhama will look after them while you wander around. Anuja needs rest and reassurance.'

'Whatever you say is fine by me.'

With that, Maya embraced Raghi and Anuja. He was not surprised that Krishna had read his mind and knew that he wanted to return home but did not quite know what to do about Raghi and Anuja. Krishna summoned the chariot. He helped Anuja and Raghi board it, and embraced Maya once more.

'Do not go back before visiting us in Dwarka once. I very much need you to see Dwarka and see me. Do not forget.'

Maya choked with emotion. He was touched by Krishna's affection. He never thought Krishna would say what he did. He knew that Krishna was not so much making a request, but telling Maya what was going to happen when his time with Takshak would be over. He bowed to Krishna. The chariot sped off back to where the boat had been.

ॐ

21

Takshak II

As Krishna left, Takshak enveloped Maya in his arms and held him tight for a long time. Maya was moved. He had not seen Takshak for some time now—maybe a year or was it more. It was before the war began, or even before then. He thanked Krishna in his heart for this favour. If he had not met Takshak, he would have left this land without saying his goodbyes.

'It is so wonderful to see you alive and well. I was worried that you may have become entangled in the stupid quarrel of those Aryas and got killed like most of them. Duryodhana had made you a king, so I thought you would fight on his side. But something, someone saved you.'

'It was their pride. They made me a king, gave me some villages, but never thought of me as anyone more than a workman. I was an artisan, a person working with his hands. I was not a Brahman or a Kshatriya. I could not be a Vaishya. So I had to be a Shudra. A king, but a Shudra all the same. So no one gave much thought to the idea of me joining the army on any side. Except for Krishna, everyone else had forgotten about me. I had built their palaces and that was the end of my usefulness.'

'For the Aryas, if you are not a Brahmin or a Kshatriya, you are a Shudra or a Danav, Daitya, Rakshasa, Mleccha. Nagas are also among the people they do not like. You do not matter. They admired you for your buildings since they had seen nothing like it. But once you had built those structures, you were forgotten. You became Maya Danav. They are proud of themselves.'

Takshak again embraced Maya as if to make sure that he was actually seeing his old friend and not caught in some dream.

'Well, I am happy that they were so proud. It was their pride which led to the battle, where they killed each other for eighteen days. I am happy that my enemies have quarrelled among themselves. It will be easy for me now to get our land back.'

'Krishna asked me to tell you that you should not take Yudhishthira lightly. He will regroup his armies and perform a Asvamedha yajna to win more territory. He told you to be more careful.'

'It might be so. I will think about it. But I have a lot of time. Nagas, my people, have been here since before these Aryas came, and we will be here after they are gone. We will get our land back, even if it takes us generations.'

'But by then, Yudhishthira will be gone and so will you. Who will fight then?'

'The next Takshak and if not him, ten Takshaks later, the Nagas will still be fighting the Aryas. We have the patience of a people who know that justice is on our side. This is our land after all. We were here before they came. There have been Takshaks before me, twenty five of them. Many more will come after me.'

As they were talking, they were walking along the streets of the town. Very few people were to be seen. It was clear to Maya that this must have been a big busy town once.

'Tell me what happened? Where are the people who lived here?'

'It is a long story. Every tale in this land began as a quarrel that went on to become an epic battle. I have many things to show you and many stories to tell. I told Krishna to bring you here because this is the nearest old city to Ghadda River, which

the Aryas call Saraswati. It used to be a very broad river, but has
shrunk now. Its story is the story of our land.'

'I saw these amazing houses and squares. Who were the people
living here?'

'Many different groups. The Nagas, of course, were here before
anyone else. The Vrishnis too were here. This is actually their old
kingdom. Our original kingdom was further up the river—not
the Ghadda, but the Sindhu. I will show you the mighty Sindhu.
Our kingdom was way up north. Its capital was called Takshila.
We had to leave it as the Aryas poured in—thousands of them,
with their cattle. So we moved away from here, went looking
for forests where we could live. Long before that, we were also
here, as this was a mix of forests and clear land. Those days, we
had struck an alliance with the Vrishnis.

The Vrishnis are cattle people who keep moving in search
of pasture. They were here many generations ago and many of
these houses belong to them. Then they went away. Shura, their
leader, Krishna's grandfather, was a clever man. He knew many
things. He could divine when the rains would not come and how
dry the land could become. Everyone said he could do magic.'

'Like Krishna?'

'Yes, and his father Vasudeva. He was taught everything by
Shura, who could see that the rains were drying up in these parts.
The grass became dry and did not last for long. The cattle were
starving. So he decided he had to take his people elsewhere. He
had an idea where, but he wanted to be sure. Vasudeva and Kunti
were both quite young then. She was just a child. But he decided
he could not leave them behind. My grandfather was sorry to
see them go. His mother's sister had married Shura's father. So
we were cousins. My grandfather told them if they did not like
where they were going, they should come back here. Krishna,
too, was told the same by his father, and, thus, they came back
here just one generation later, but went down to Dwarka. The
Vrishnis are very willing to pull out from one place and plant

their roots in a new country, if need be.'

Maya was getting to hear a new story about the land where he had been living for many years now. He had no idea that Krishna, who was not of the same people as the Aryas, was still worshipped by them.

'So, was this the capital of their kingdom?'

'No. Their capital was further down towards where the sun sets. It is by the Sindhu, which you have to see. Let us get into my chariot.'

Maya was overwhelmed by what he was witnessing. There were structures everywhere—public baths, meeting places, houses. But very few people were to be seen. Where had they all gone?

'So, why is no one living here?'

'The rains began to fail. The climate dried up. Grass disappeared. Before that, many communities lived together peacefully here. The Vrishnis had their cattle. We, the Nagas, liked dense forests. There were the Dravida people, with smooth brown skins and dark black hair, who were good at trading. They sailed out to places in the direction of where the sun rises.

We all came, one after another, from a densely forested area, not far away if you sail the other way where the sun sets. That place began to get crowded and so my people, who like forests, came here in boats. Vrishnis realized that what we had done was their future too. So they followed us. As the Vrishnis cleared the land for their cattle, we moved where there were forests and tall grass still. We eat any small creature that moves, and do not really need houses to live in. The Vrishnis were good to us and helped us move up to where the forests were. We had intermarriages. Krishna must have told you about the Naga princess in his family.'

'Yes, he did. But the Vrishnis came back.'

'The Magadhis did not like them coming in. Shura made alliances with everyone. He was a shrewd man. He knew the Vrishnis were not the ones to fight—they just wanted land for their cattle. So he made friends with the Aryas by giving his daughter away for adoption. He also got his son Vasudeva married to Kamsa's sister. Kamsa was a suspicious man. He thought Vasudeva might betray him. The Aryas wanted to come in where the Magadhis were. You must have heard Krishna talk about Jarasandha and Sishupal.'

'Yes, he did.'

'Krishna is one of the cleverest people I know. He knew Vrishnis could not fight the Magadhis. So, like his grandfather and father, he became friends with the Aryas. He chose Kunti's sons because she was a Vrishni and his aunt.'

'I had heard that he helped them when they were wandering in disguise.'

'Yes. Krishna championed them because they needed help to get their due. The land of the two rivers is the most fertile and the Aryas were hungry for good land to spread their people. The Magadhis were not happy with this. Krishna helped the Aryas by arranging for Arjuna to win Draupadi. That helped them claim their portion.'

'So what were we doing in that forest that Krishna had burned down?'

'The Aryas had thrown us out of the forest, which is just up the river here. So we were moving like the Vrishnis towards the two big rivers, seeking forests to live in. The Aryas built their huts, but when many of them started coming in from beyond the mountains they had to build towns. Not like what you will see here, they were smaller.'

Takshak stopped the chariot. They had arrived at what was the biggest river Maya had seen, even bigger than the Ganga. There was a boat waiting for them. Takshak helped Maya board and signalled the sailors to move. Maya realized that they were crossing the river to the other side. Maya could see that it was a deep river with a strong current. Soon, they managed to cross over.

There was another chariot waiting for them. Maya thought he recognized the charioteer, but could not quite recall who he was. Takshak saw the puzzled look on Maya's face. The charioteer bowed low to Maya.

'Remember him? You were last together in a burning forest.'

Maya said, 'Ashvasena? You look so different. How long has it been? What have you been doing?'

Maya hugged Ashvasena. He kept on looking at him, almost examining the person before him and trying to understand how he had changed. He was also draped with a serpent around his neck, much like his father. Maya had not seen him for nearly fifteen years.

'Krishna and Arjuna carried you away, but this boy had to get out on his own that day. Luckily, he knew the route to escape.'

'That was so many moons ago. I had already built the palace and the Pandavas had gone away in exile then.'

'Then they came back and killed one another.'

'Yes, but as Krishna told me, that was dharma'.

'I love dharma. Aryas kill each other and call it their duty. It makes our life easy.'

Maya noticed that the chariot was going uphill. In fact, ever since he left Anuja and Raghi, he had been travelling uphill. There were hills all around, with plateaus. Ashvasena seemed to be familiar with the surroundings. He drove the chariot till they arrived in what seemed like a large town square. This was much larger than the previous place they had been to, where he had met Takshak. Indeed, the entire surroundings, with all the buildings, roads and canals were larger than anything Maya had ever seen before. He realized that this was the place his father must have heard of. But how?

Maya had not noticed that Ashvasena had disappeared as soon as he had gotten off the chariot. Now he was coming back, almost running. He was holding something in his hands very carefully. As soon as Ashvasena removed the cloth covering what he was carrying, Maya could not believe his eyes. This was something he had not seen since he left his home many years ago. There were pieces of maize corn roasted to a fine brown colour, served on a copper plate.

'Father said you liked these,' Asvasena said with a knowing smile.

'Where did you get these from? I have been thinking about these for years. I never thought I would see them till I reached home.'

Takshak had been silently watching Maya, enjoying his reaction.

'Remember Xa'tum? Once he knew you were from Maya, he wanted you to build him something. Rotolu was the same. I met you on Rotolu's island—we all hail from a large Naga family. Their people travelled farther in boats from where we all were. Our families stopped quite near from where we all come from. It is a land not far away from here. They decided they would find somewhere else. They are sailors and travel long distances. Xa'tum told me about your home, what you people ate and how you worshipped the serpent. You are just a Naga, one of us.'

Maya saw that Takshak was not far from the truth. Takshak did not have the red hair he had, but did have the same skin colour and build. By now, he was enjoying his corn too much to worry about anything else.

'When the rains started failing, the people, who used to live where we are going, found that this was the best crop to feed themselves. What remained could be fed to their cattle. They call it makka. Would you like some more?'

'Later, perhaps. I have to look at this bath. Was it where they met to worship?'

'They came here every day. Those from other communities would come for full moon nights and on other special days. There would be crowds of people looking up at the moon. You see these passages around? Water would flow into them from larger tanks, which we will see. It was a get-together, a worship, a celebration, when it came to having a bath together. There would be carts full of food all around and people had jugs of soma prepared. It would go on all night.'

'This reminds me of my home,' Maya said.

'This was the town where three different communities gathered on full moon nights. There was no king as such, but each community had a big family. The big families would look after their people. This is how Shura's mother was also a Naga, as the Vrishnis and Nagas often intermarried. We had to live in peace together.'

Maya looked at the passages built for water to flow into the public bath. Asvasena was guiding him around the square, which had the public bath and also the tall buildings around. These were bigger than the palaces he had built for the Pandavas and Kauravas. These structures were tight together, with not much space between them.

'We started building reservoirs for water once we saw how precious it was. The rains were fine when our people came here, but then we had just a few spurts of rainfall and then nothing for long. So these baths also were used as underground water storage. We began to bathe together as a ritual and that also helped maintain friendly relations.'

Their walk had brought them to a building with a large wall. It was like a palace—the sort his father used to build back home. Takshak led them in. They climbed up some steps and went behind a door. There stood a woman smiling at Maya.

'How many years has it been since I saw you last?'

Maya recalled. This was the woman who was looking after him in that house in Khandava forest. It was Shukri, Takshak's wife.

'Though Krishna and Arjuna carried me away, it was you who saved me. You had shouted something to Krishna, but I have no idea what it was.'

'You were not only immersed in working with your toy buildings but also intoxicated because of that favourite plant of yours that you were chewing. You did not know where you were.'

'That is right. I had no idea that Takshak had left us and gone away. I thought he would protect me. But I am glad that you did.'

'It was Krishna who saved us as he understood what I was saying. Arjuna knew nothing about what I was trying to say. I had to take Asva and get him out of the fire as well. Luckily, we all survived.'

Takshak was watching their delight at meeting again. He put an arm around each of them and led them into the next room. It was a large room, obviously meant for feasts. There were a lot of bowls and plates laid around. Maya could see that these earthen plates and bowls were exquisitely decorated. He could see some corn being roasted. Shukri had clearly gone to a lot of trouble to make sure their friend would have a memorable day.

'So will you be going back home from here?' Shukri asked.

'Yes, I must go. I have been here much too long. When Takshak brought me here, I thought I would see the buildings and palaces I had come to learn about, but instead I ended up building palaces myself. Those palaces led to a long battle.'

'Do not blame yourself. They had been quarrelling from their childhood days. Had it not been because of the palaces, they would have found something else to fight about.'

'I would have left when the Pandavas went into exile. But then I had not seen these buildings. And when Duryodhana asked me to build him a palace, I could not refuse him. Then I went in search of these old buildings, but took the wrong direction. No one had told me where to go. Even Krishna did not tell me.'

Takshak could not resist. 'Krishna thought it was your dharma to spend these years in exile from your home.'

'No, he was busy. Once the Pandavas went in exile, he came to Dwarka and told me to make sure his people were safe and happy. They had walked across the land twice in two generations. He was their guardian. He made Dwarka a new home for the Vrishnis. I had not seen him for all these years till he turned up at the house I was living in. It was the house of Sudev, who I had worked with. He was a fine stonemason, one of the best.

But then he died young, and I began to look after Raghi and their daughter Anuja.'

'Where are they?'

'Krishna took them with him to Dwarka to get Anuja some rest. He said Rukmini and Satyabhama will look after them.'

'And if not them, there are many more queens who bow to Krishna's wishes,' Shukri said.

'Will they go back with you to your home?'

'That is a question that is troubling me. I have become attached to both of them. But then this is their home. If they come with me, they will have to learn new things.'

Takshak had an answer.

'You learned new things here and they can do the same. We can live anywhere if we have the people with us who we can trust.'

Shukri agreed.

'Raghi trusts you. Now that most men in Aryavarta have died, she has no one else here. Anuja is still young and will find a suitable husband in your land. I am not a Naga. When the Dravid people began to leave this land and sailed away, my father did not go with them. They were traders, but he was a priest. He wanted to go on living here, where he built little statues and gave them to people for worshipping. So we stayed behind. The Nagas were still here, and that is how I became one of them.'

Shukri made a sign to Asva. He got up and left the room. Takshak could see that Maya wanted to take Raghi and Anuja with him.

'As I said before, this area has always had different communities. We did not worry about high and low. We spoke each other's language. We knew we had all come from somewhere and may end up elsewhere. Like Shura and the Vrishnis, the Dravidas left, but they found somewhere better to settle and hence did not come back.'

Asva came back into the room carrying a straw basket and

put it beside Shukri. She took out small clay figures from the basket and handed them to Maya. He was astonished. There were images of animals and people finely etched in clay.

'My father would spend days on end working on one of these. He had to find the right kind of clay—neither too soft, nor too hard. He moulded it but still left it malleable. Then he would take his copper tongs, heat them and begin to etch little shapes—bull, bird, human face—very carefully, as the mould could easily break. Making one small figure like this would take him several days. Sometimes, they broke before he had even finished. But once they were ready, people wanted them.'

Shukri laid out many such small animal and human figures. Maya picked up one after another, fascinated by the etchings on such small surfaces.

'Many of his little figures used to be taken by our relatives who were traders. They would go across the land over the hills, where there are big towns and sell my father's etchings. Some took them when they went sailing up and down the Sindhu. That was how they knew that when things got bad here and the rains failed, they could sail and go south.'

Takshak said to Asva, 'Go find those necklaces grandfather made.'

Maya was still busy admiring the etchings. He noted one made of stone, which was rather soft and was something he had never seen before.

'Did people wear them or did they worship them?'

'They carried them for good luck. The idea was that if you held one in your palm, you would get what you wished for.'

'Did it work?'

'They came back and wanted more, so who knows. Maybe they did. Take some and try.'

Takshak saw the drift of Shukri's idea.

'You are going to need all the luck for sailing for many moon cycles till you reach home. Take one for yourself and two for Raghi and Anuja.'

Asva came in and handed a small bundle to Shukri, which was carrying a stunningly beautiful necklace. Maya could see it was made of gold and had seven small discs, each thin and round, strung together with a silver chain.

'My mother made that. She would cook and feed us all, and then when we children would go to bed, she would start work on each gold leaf and then on the silver string. Then, they had to be strung together.'

'Did she ever wear it?'

'No. She always believed that if you wear something precious that you made yourself, then bad luck will hit you.'

'Have you?'

'No. I am waiting.'

'For?'

'A chance to give it away.'

'To?'

'Maybe Asva's wife, if he ever gets married.'

Takshaka knew that this was a conversation his son did not want to engage in. So he said, 'Come, let us eat. Shukri has prepared a feast for you. I do not know what you've had to eat on the boat all these days. You have to see what her people ate over the many years. Shukri wants to tell you the story of the Dravidas.'

ನಾಣಿ

22

The King II

Yudhishthira was feeling happy and cheerful. He smiled looking at the sleeping maiden, who was probably having happy dreams. It had been a pleasant encounter. She was beautiful. He had been good to her. She liked to be in the palace and in the beautiful, big bedchamber. It had been well decorated and smelled of fragrant flowers. She had refused his offer of soma, but held up the cup for him to drink as she clung close to him.

Now he had to attend to his many tasks of the long day. He put a silken sheet on her and left the chamber. Once outside, he instructed the women to look after the maiden and ensure that she got back home safely. It was still very early in the day, the hour before sunrise. He had to bathe and perform his rituals. He had to propitiate the ancestors and make offerings to the gods.

As he descended into the pool of water, which had been prepared the way he liked it—with water neither too hot, nor cold—he began to enjoy the gentle massage being given by his maid. There was another pouring in fresh pots of water. There was a chanting of mantras, which could be heard coming from the small temple next to the pool.

Yudhishthira had begun to feel like the king he always wanted to be. Sadly, Bhishma was gone. He had given Yudhishthira a lot of good advice. But once he was assured that Uttara's foetus was safe and there was no danger of the Kuru line ending, Bhishma agreed on giving up his life. Draupadi had been very cheerful lately, more than she had been for years. She was lively when she was with him, cheering him up, submitting gladly. It was once again like their early years of marriage. It must be that Draupadi had been keeping them all happy as his brothers were less gloomy than they had been immediately after the war. Draupadi had also been looking after Uttara and making sure the child in the womb was safe. He was to become the king, with no one above him.

He decided to luxuriate in the bath a bit longer.

တာ

23

Draupadi: The Happy One

D raupadi was still asleep. She now made sure to come and sleep in Uttara's room once the husband she was with had fallen asleep. Normally, she would lie in his arms and feel his body near her. But now, checking on Uttara every night had become her priority. It was also her secret pleasure, as she knew that her child with Arjuna was safe in Uttara's womb. She wanted to make sure that the child was born safe and strong.

Uttara had been surprised by this love. Ever since Abhimanyu had lost his life, she had felt lonely and miserable. She was far from her own family and knew no one here. Before she could become part of the family, Abhimanyu had died. Then she found out she was carrying his child, after which the family refused to let her go back to her old home. She was lonely and miserable. She had become very sick, nearly losing her child. That was a dreadful time. The elders kept on coming to see her and that made her even more miserable. It was not her but the baby she carried that they were interested in.

But then Draupadi began to visit regularly. She shared her memories of being a young bride in a large household. She told Uttara how she had not been prepared to have five husbands, but could not disobey Kunti. They were in their palace in Indraprastha only for a short time—that was the only happy phase of her life. When they lost the game, her misery returned. For thirteen years, she kept her hair loose, wore no fine clothes and did not feel cheerful. She told Uttara that once her child was born, she would be able to have her life back.

It was the early hours of the morning. Uttara was awake and saw that Draupadi was still asleep. She had a smile on her lips. Uttara looked at her and once again realized how incredibly beautiful Draupadi was. No wonder the beauty had divided the family and caused a war. And what for? There she was, all her sons killed, her brother and father killed as well. What did she have to look forward to?

Draupadi felt those young eyes on her and woke up smiling. She draped her arms around Uttara and brought her closer to herself.

'How are you feeling this morning?'

'Fine. It is getting bigger and heavier.'

'That is what we all want. A big strong boy.'

'I try not to think about the future. I fear it may bring bad luck.'

'No. Don't think like that. You have nothing to worry about. Krishna will protect you. He is your uncle, a friend as well as our protector. Have faith in him. He will take care of you.'

'You are his sister and you are taking care of me. Who else do I need?'

Draupadi hugged Uttara a bit tighter. Things were going to be alright. Her son was safe. She thanked Vyasa and Krishna silently.

৩৩

24

Krishna in Dwarka

The remaining journey to Dwarka did not take long for Raghi and Anuja. Krishna took good care of Anuja, and made sure they were well protected and fed. When they reached their destination, there was a chariot waiting for them, which drove them to Dwarka. Daruka, Krishna's charioteer, was pleased to see his master. He had stayed behind in Dwarka, while Krishna himself had become Arjuna's charioteer.

Anuja was amazed to see the big city they had come to. It was bigger than Hastinapur where she had grown up. The palace they drove to was just one among a cluster. Raghi was worried that being in another palace may bring the bad memories of that night in Anuja's mind. But Krishna was, as ever, very caring.

As soon as they arrived, Rukmini and Satyabhama came bearing garlands. They touched Krishna's feet and put garlands around his neck. He embraced them, fondly kissing them. Then they garlanded Raghi and Anuja with flowers, and hugged them. Soon, there were other queens coming to greet Krishna and garlanding them.

Krishna said to Satyabhama, 'These are our honoured guests. We have to look after them. We have been travelling for days, and they need rest and some food.'

Satyabhama led them away to another part of the palace.

Rukmini went with Krishna to their private wing in the palace. Anuja kept looking at the big rooms and the decorations of gold and silver. There were silken draperies and curtains everywhere. People, mostly women, were milling about, now happy that Krishna was back. Satyabhama stopped near a room and opened the doors. It was a large bedroom with two large beds. There were places to sit with cushions, golden jugs of water and collection of sweets. There were flowers everywhere.

Satyabhama said, 'Consider this your home. Rest here, and then, whenever you want anything, just ask. I will send some women who will look after you. If you need to find me, just ask the servants. They will guide you.'

Satyabhama hurried back to where Krishna was. As she had expected, he was seated happily, surrounded by seven women, all his queens. He was reclined on a bed with large cushions holding Kalindi in his right arm by her slim waist; Mitravanda was on his left with her fingers running through his hair; Jambuvati was sitting on the large seat massaging his feet, while Nagnajiti could not resist touching him and stroking him. He drew Lakshana near him, holding her hand. Bhadra was gently massaging his head, while Rukmini was caressing him. This was his way to keep them happy, and happy they were, with no one jealous of another. It was their love for Krishna that Rukmini and Satyabhama amicably stayed together.

They all just wanted to touch him, hear his voice and look at him. They had not seen him for such a long time. He had gone away to negotiate a truce, but that had failed. Then the war had lasted eighteen days. Even after that, Krishna had stayed back to settle Yudhishthira as the new king. Now, at last, he was among his women, and they were all aching to be close to him.

Krishna was also happy to be back among his favourite women. He loved them all, each in his own way, and how each wished to be loved. He had a thousand ways of pleasing women. He had known these arts since his childhood days in Gokul.

Thinking of Gokul, he remembered Radha—the way she had surprised him, the few moments they had spent together and her quick disappearance. The burden of caring for others was getting heavier. For a moment, a cloud passed over his face.

Satyabhama saw this and moved closer to him. She took his face in her hands and kissed him full on the mouth deeply and for long. Before he could say anything, she invited the others to follow her example. Soon, Krishna was being hugged, kissed and smothered by lips and mouths caressing him, uttering soft words, some even sobbing with happiness. And yet he was not fully there.

Satyabhama said, 'My sweet lord, why this dark cloud over your mind? I see that something is worrying you. How can we remove that cloud? Command us and we are here to give ourselves to make you happy.'

Krishna replied, 'Yes, there is something worrying me, but I am trying to think what it is. Here among my loving beautiful women, whom I have not seen for a long time, I am troubled. I wish I knew why.'

A knock on the door interrupted their conversation. This was unusual, as this was a private wing in Krishna's palace. But the knock was impatient. Krishna knew at once. It was Balarama, his older brother. Rukmini, too, realized who it was. It had to be urgent if Balarama had come so soon after Krishna's arrival. She knew him to be a stern person, not known to be diverted by anyone's charms. She was about to take the women away, but Krishna stopped her. He went to the doors and there was Balarama, his face red with anger.

Krishna bowed and touched his feet. He shut the doors behind him and began walking with Balarama in the corridor of the palace. Balarama was still fuming. Krishna put his arms around his brother's shoulder.

'What is it, brother? I have not seen you for such a long time. What worries you? Tell me.'

'It is our young men. They are out of control. They will bring ruin on us.'

'What has happened?'

'They have insulted Maharshis Kanva, Vishwamitra and Narada.'

'What have they done?'

'The Maharshis came earlier today. They had heard you were about to arrive. They bathed in the sea and were deep in their samadhi. One of the young men, your son Samba, I am told, was dressed up like a pregnant woman. He was taken by the others to the Maharshis, where they sought their blessings so that he could bear many children.'

'Then?'

'Vishwamitra said, "What he will bear will destroy you all."'

Krishna now realized that it was not Radha and her worries that had been bothering him, but Vyasa warning him of what was happening.

'I must go and fall at the feet of the maharshis and ask for forgiveness.'

'Do you think that will help?'

'I have to, if only to save our boys.'

'Do you think they deserve saving?'

'But they are our boys. My son, Samba. We have to save them.'

'You did not save the Aryas from killing each other. Are our boys any different for you?'

Krishna was thunderstruck. This was what Maya had given him an earful about too. Why had he not saved the Aryas, but ensured his own people escaped unhurt. What and where was his dharma?

Balarama continued.

'Remember, I went away while they were fighting at Kurukshetra because I did not want them to fight. I did not want you to help them fight. I did not like you helping the Pandavas. You helped them break the rules. I saw it myself. I had come back from my yatra, when on the last day you helped

Bhima cheat and kill Duryodhana.'

'What do you order me to do? You are my older brother. I will obey your command.'

'I will not command you. The world is overburdened with bad deeds. My time here is up. I am going to ask the sea to take me to its bosom. You can do what you think is right.'

Saying that, Balarama walked away and out of the palace.

Krishna stood there for a while. Not often in his life had he been so perplexed. What was he to do? He saw Rukmini coming towards him, looking worried. He needed to soothe her. This was his problem, not hers or of any of the other queens. Krishna had to keep them happy. He saw a woman standing by waiting to help. He said to her, 'Tell Daruka to come here as soon as he can.'

The woman bowed and began running to the outer doors of the palace.

Rukmini asked, 'What was it, my lord?'

'Maharshi Kanva, Vishwamitra and Narada are here. I will ask Daruka to fetch them and look after them.'

'Shall I?'

'No. All of you have to look after me tonight.'

Rukmini saw the mischief in Krishna's eyes. She put her arms around his neck and tiptoed to kiss him. *This is what he means*, she thought. She was right, as Krishna held on to her tight. He had made up his mind. Maya was right and so was Balarama. He could not save the Vrishnis if he had let the Aryas die. He had to bear the burden of dharma. He would not ask Vishwamitra to relent. Justice had to be done. But tonight his place was by the side of his women, who had given their best years to him. The world can wait.

'Maharshi Vishwamitra, Kanva and Narada are here. Find them and bring them to the palace, and put them at ease. Tell them I have just arrived and am resting. I will see them early in the morning.'

Daruka went away running to his chariot.

Krishna turned Rukmini around and grabbed her from the

back holding her in a tight grip. It had been a long time. She began walking back, but Krishna held her tight. She let him be the master. Embracing each other like newly-weds, they came back in the room where the others were waiting.

They surrounded him again.

'We all want what you gave to Rukmini,' Kalindi said.

'Why not? But there is only one problem.'

'What is that?' Jambuvati asked.

'I cannot decide who to take first.'

'We are happy for you to choose whoever you like the best,' Bhadra added.

'I like you all equally. When I am with one, I am thinking of the others.'

Lakshana saw that Krishna was playing a game to last the night. She said, 'We will blindfold you. You have to chase us. When you catch one, you have to tell who it is. If you love us all, you should be able to tell.'

'And if I do?'

'She will give you whatever garment you demand of her. And then she will tell you who to go to next.'

'But what if I don't get it right?'

'Then you have to give her whatever she demands and become her slave.'

'Fine. I gain whether I lose or win.'

'No. We gain,' said Nagnajiti.

It was soon a swirling, screaming laughing game. Krishna wandered about and grabbed each in turn. They let him kiss them and fondle them. Soon the dresses were cast on the floor. Krishna was taking one after another. They wanted to be caught, and soon he was deep into the arms of Mitravanda, who demanded that she be the first of the night to have him.

This was going to be a night of Krishna Leela for them. Krishna knew there may not be another night after this.

25

Maya in Heaven

Maya was in heaven. At last, he had come to the place he wanted to visit. He had seen a lot the previous day, but now was up again in the early hours looking around. He wanted to look at each building carefully through the eyes of a builder. He wanted to grasp the techniques used to build tall structures, the different materials used, the design and the layout of the town squares. This required time and concentration. Takshak knew Maya wanted to be left on his own. He had other things to do and so he let him be. Asva, in any case, was not an early morning person.

To show Maya the other sites, Takshak had to make preparations. He thought that Maya should go up north with him and be nearer to the mountains, which fed the rivers. Many generations ago, the Nagas were in the forests of that region. Takshila, the capital, was there. Now it had been overrun by the Aryas, who had also taken over what they called Gandhara.

But Takshak had to be ready for Maya's long journey. He was sure Krishna would arrange for a ship, which will be able to take Maya and the two women back all the way to where he had come from. He had to be provided with food and clothing and the things that would help in case the ship foundered. Of course, there were Rotolu and X'atum to help. The Nagas were scattered along the entire way.

Suddenly, Takshak felt uneasy. He was not quite sure why. It was then that he realized that Krishna was trying to commune with him. Takshak sat down on the ground and concentrated. It was indeed Krishna. He had just one message: *Bring Maya here as soon as possible.* Takshak called Shukri. She heard the urgency in his voice.

'What is it, Takshak?'

'We have to get Maya ready for departure.'

'I thought you were going to eat here and then get into your boat to go to Takshila.'

'No. Krishna has asked to get Maya to Dwarka as soon as possible. There seems to be a major problem or Krishna would not be calling him.'

'I better pack food and presents.'

'What are you planning?'

'I want him to take what we showed him last night. He was fascinated by those clay figures. He should have them.'

'And the necklace?'

'Yes. Maybe he can give it to Anuja.'

'Good. I better go find him.'

Takshak went out to the big bath they had taken Maya to the previous day. He found him deep at the bottom examining the paths through which the water came in. He was measuring the width of certain walls with his arms, examining the brickwork very carefully.

Maya saw Takshak and said, 'This is so useful for me. I am learning so much. I wish I had been here earlier. Have you come to take me to the other town?'

'No. I have to take you to Krishna. Something has happened and he wants to see you as soon as possible.'

'Has Anuja suffered another shock? Is Raghi alright?'

'It is not about them as far as I can know. Krishna was talking about something more serious that he wishes to tell you.'

'When do we go?'

'As soon as you are ready.'

'Let us go.'

They went back into the house where Shukri and Asva were. Shukri had wrapped up the clay figurines and the necklace. Maya gathered his own goods, which he had brought for his short journey. They descended from the palace and headed towards the chariot. Maya was surprised when Shukri got into the boat with them.

'Are you also coming with us?'

'I want to meet Anuja and Raghi before they go away to your distant land.'

'Leaving poor Asva alone?'

'He is delighted to be left alone,' Takshak said.

Maya kept looking back at the buildings he was leaving behind. He had seen some spectacular structures in the two towns they had stopped in. His experienced eyes had taken in a lot. Now, all he had to do was to get back, settle in Raghi and Anuja and get to work.

The Sindhu was friendly now. They were, anyway, heading downstream. Maya knew it would not take very long. Why did Krishna call him back so soon?

ಌಌ

26

The Curse

Krishna woke up quite early. As he looked around, his women were fast asleep, replete and happy with the night's pleasures. He kept on looking. Each had her own beauty and a distinct character. They had given him so much happiness. But he knew that it was all coming to an end. Ever since that night with Radha, he felt his burden get increasingly heavier. His guru Sandipani had warned him. His father Vasudeva had toughened him for his life. He had fought so many battles, killed evil men, tackled large serpents, lifted mountains, led his people back from Gokul to Dwarka, helped the Pandavas win their kingdom and save their kula from destruction at the hands of their enemies.

But he had come to think that it was time to stop. That brief night with Radha had taught him that his life would always be for others, never for himself. When Vyasa had conveyed Draupadi's request and he had to refuse her, he was in despair. He knew what he wanted to do, but could not, owing to his higher responsibility—preserving the order.

He walked out of the room, leaving the queens asleep and went into the pool for a quick bath. The attendant gave him a gentle massage, which made him feel better. There was no time to linger. He thanked the attendant and got out. He changed quickly and walked across to the wing of the palace where the maharshis awaited.

They were up, of course, deep in samadhi. They could see that Krishna was coming to meet them. Krishna came and bowed down to them. They blessed him and bowed to him in return.

'Tapasvis, I welcome you to Dwarka. I heard of the terrible offence committed by the young boys. I apologize on their behalf. I await your judgement.'

'Jewel of the Shura clan! We are pleased that you have come to see us. You have guarded dharma for many years now and kept the earth on an even keel. Your virtuous actions are many. We honour you for those good deeds,' Vishwamitra said.

'What those insolent youths did was a gross breach of good behaviour. We got angry and cursed them. Indeed, we have cursed the Vrishnis. But you are a mahayogi. You can ask us to rethink our judgement. Is that what you wish?'

'I have not come to seek mercy for those young men who insulted you or for all the young men who have lost respect for tapasya. But I do ask you to spare the women and the elderly. Let there be no young man, unmarried, married or even a father, stay alive among the Vrishnis. But let the children, the grandfathers and the women live.'

'We admire your resolve. We can see you want to save those who played no part in the disrespect shown to us. But what about the future of the Vrishnis?' It was Narada who spoke thus.

'Holy one, as long as there is even one single young woman alive who can carry a child in her belly, the Vrishnis will survive.'

'You are known around the three worlds for your firm resolve and your great deeds. But today, you have surpassed them all. You have accepted the total destruction of young Vrishni men when you could have asked us to reverse our curse. You have not saved even your own sons,' Vishwamitra said.

'Or you could have reversed our curse yourself. You have the chakra, which would shatter the iron club which the boy would give birth to. Why did you not do that?' Kanva said.

'Mahamunis, when the earth is heavy with evil doers, it is our duty to reduce her burden.'

'These are indeed noble words. We salute your sacrifice and bow down to you.'

'We are honoured that you decided to visit Dwarka. Come again whenever you wish. Kindly grant me permission to go now.'

'You have our permission,' all three chanted.

Krishna walked away slowly. His heart was heavy. Those words of Maya and then of Balarama had stung him. Maya had challenged the very idea of dharma and Balarama had woken him up by telling him that compassion for one and death for another would not do. He had been cruel to Draupadi and kind to Uttara. It was Maya who saved him from being cruel to Anuja by refusing to follow his way of resolving the King's difficulty. He needed to talk to Maya. Where was he? He concentrated for a while and located Takshak. The latter promised to bring Maya to Dwarka as soon as possible.

As Krishna walked away, somber in his thoughts, he found Narada rushing towards him. Krishna was surprised; he had just taken leave of the mahamunis. *What did Narada want to say now?*

Krishna stopped and again bowed low. Narada was smiling.

'Dharmaraja told me you helped rescue his kingdom from great trouble.'

'I just did what I could to help him in his plight.'

'I gather Quetl was of great help. He is a nice boy.'

'Quetl?' Krishna asked.

'You call him Maya Raja. But his name is Quetl.'

'Mahamuni, how do you know him?'

'I met him while travelling across the five oceans. He was building a big statue of Naga. I saw his palm and knew he would come among us.'

'Mahamuni, you truly know about the many worlds and have visited them. I salute you.'

'You have chosen well. You have my blessings.'

Krishna wanted to ask Narada how he knew what he had chosen, but he had disappeared by then.

Puzzled over what Narada said, Krishna knew he had a lot of work to do and very little time. He first went to see his parents. Vasudeva and Devaki had been in Dwarka from the day they had all come back from Gokul. They were happy there, looking after the large family of daughters-in-law, sons and grandchildren.

Vasudeva was pleased to see Krishna. Devaki was in tears as she embraced her son, whom she had not seen for many days. Vasudeva could see that Krishna was in a sombre mood.

'What is on your mind?'

'Death and destruction. The young men of Dwarka have insulted Maharshis Vishwamitra, Kanva and Narada, and have been cursed by them to die. Do not go outside in the city. Stay here and guard everyone.'

'Are you not going into the city to stop them?'

'No. This time they have exceeded the limits. There are evils which must be punished.'

'Tell Samba and Pradyumna to stay in.'

'It is too late for that.'

'Where is Balrama?'

'He was so angry that he decided to go and immerse himself into the sea. He believes Kaliyuga is already here and he does not want to live any longer.'

Devaki started sobbing loudly. 'I will run to him and stop him. I will beg him to stay for our sake.'

'It is too late for that. He went last night. I must go. There is much to do.'

'What are you going to do?'

'I do not know yet.'

Krishna knew he had to tell his queens what was about to happen. He did not know himself what he wanted to do, but he had to look after them. He had to tell Jambuvati that her son

Samba had been among the main troublemakers. Rukmini had to be told about the fate awaiting Pradyumna. It was going to be difficult to decide who else to tell and how to tell.

Then he remembered. He had to check on Raghi and Anuja. He went back to the palace and entered Satyabhama's room. She was up and had got ready for the day. Krishna felt a pang of desire as he looked at Satyabhama. She herself was surprised to see him so early in the morning. Normally, she would wait till he summoned her as they all had to allow each other their own time with Krishna.

She rushed to him and bowed. He lifted her up and kissed her fondly. Satyabhama sensed that Krishna was in a sombre mood. But he often was when the cares of the world were on his mind.

'My lord, what can I do to lighten your burden?'

Krishna was once again impressed by how quickly Satyabhama had sensed his mood.

'I need to find Raghi and Anuja. Maya is arriving tonight.'

'I thought he was taking his time going around the old towns with Takshak. Has he changed his mind?'

'No, I have. Let us meet them and then I will tell you.'

Satyabhama realized that something major had befallen them. She thought again about last night and about that knock on the door.

Satyabhama hugged Krishna, but this time with sadness. Krishna kissed her deeply for a long time. They walked in silence to where Raghi and Anuja were. Anuja had been up and was dressed, ready to head out. She was surprised to see Krishna, and bowed low and touched his feet. Raghi too was taken aback to see Krishna and bowed.

'I do hope you have been comfortable here,' Krishna said.

'Yes, my lord. They have looked after us very well. We were just thinking of asking them if we could go and see your beautiful city.'

'Dwarka is in a state of turmoil. I would urge you to stay in the palace. Maya is arriving tonight and he will be ready to take you with him on your long journey. So please ask the women to prepare everything for you that you will require. They will get it ready.'

'Will we be leaving tonight?'

'That is Maya's plan.'

Krishna knew he was reversing who had said what to whom, but the message was still the same.

Krishna left with Satyabhama. After they had walked past two rooms, he opened the doors to a room and took her in. Satyabhama understood. He wanted them to be all alone. Krishna shut the door behind him. He took her hand and sat her down on his lap. He kissed her again, but with an infinite sadness.

'What is it, my lord?'

'The young men of the Vrishnis have invited ruin on Dwarka. We are going to lose them all today as they will fight and kill each other.'

'Can you not stop them?'

'No. I am not stopping them. They have subverted dharma and insulted Mahamunis Vishwamitra, Kana and Narada. I cannot save them.'

'All the young men?'

'Yes. How do I tell Rukmini and Jambuvati?'

'Samba?'

'Yes. He was the leader of the disrespectful crowd.'

'Pradyumna too?'

'He got caught in the troubles that flared up.'

Satyabhama saw Krishna was tired in a way she had never seen him be before. She clasped him to her bosom and stroked his head gently. She knew that a bridge had been crossed. She had to be the strong one.

'You rest. I will bring them all here.'

Krishna looked at Satyabhama with pride and admiration. She was as strong as she was beautiful. He had to decide what he was to tell them. Whichever way he said it, it was going to be painful. But then, this was finally his burden and no one else's. He decided to sit in samadhi for a while.

Satyabhama brought Jambuvati and Rukmini first, and then went out again to get the others. She had warned them that there was sombre news to be shared. Rukmini sat on the left of Krishna and Jambuvati on the right. Krishna kissed Jambuvati first. He took her in his lap and folded her into his arms.

'We have lost our son Samba.'

Jambuvati could not believe what she had heard. She broke into a loud sob. Rukmini got up and put her arm on her back and soothed her. But Jambuvati was inconsolable.

Krishna drew Rukmini to her and said, 'And our son Pradyumna.'

Rukmini was stoic. She had expected this once Satyabhama had told her how sad Krishna was. She was one of the main queens. She had to be brave and look after the others. She kept on stroking Jambuvati's back.

Soon the others had come in. They were all aware that unlike the previous evening, this was a bridge into the unknown future. Krishna got up from his throne and gently put Jambuvati on it. He took Rukmini's hand, brought her nearer and kissed her, but with great sadness. He did the same with Kalindi, Nagnajiti, Bhargi, Mitravanda, Lakshana and Satyabhama.

He said, 'Kaliyuga has begun. Our young men treated three maharshis with disrespect and in turn were cursed by them. All our young men are to die fighting with each other, intoxicated with pride. I asked the maharshis to forgive Dwarka and the Vrishnis, but not the young men. So for a while, there will be only women, children and the elderly.

All my life, I have tried to uphold dharma, thinking of the need to preserve the order and respect the learned. The only time I have been able to fight the burden is when I have been with women who have given me their infinite love. All of you

have made me the happiest man whenever I have been with
you. But I must go now, and I wanted to tell you and you alone
what I am doing.'

There was loud sobbing as everyone rushed forward to touch
him. Some fell at his feet, others tried to clasp him. He knew
he had to be strong-hearted.

Kalindi was the first to speak.

'My lord, we see no joy in life if you leave us behind. Your life
is our life. Take us with you to whichever world you are going.'

Nagnajiti agreed, 'You won me and I am yours. I do not
exist if taken apart from you. Take me too.'

Krishna let them all speak, and hug and kiss him; he stroked
their backs to console them. He had to be strong.

'Dwarka needs you as do the many elders and children. Other
women who have lost their sons and husbands will come to you
for consolation. The clan of Vrishnis will grow again and you
will be the rulers who will make it possible. Do as I tell you.'

Satyabhama said, 'My lord, we will abide by your word. But
you must listen to us. You have to stay with us because if you
are not with us, we will not be able to live.'

Rukmini said, 'You told me of the pure love shared between
you and Radha since you both were children, though you never
met her again after you left Gokul. We are your other Radhas.
Give us something, a part of you, which we can keep with us.'

Krishna was moved once again at the mere mention of Radha.
Of course, Radha was the answer to his dilemma. He always
carried her with him in his heart.

'Whenever you wish, just think of me and I will be with
you. Say my name or recall an incident together and whisper
my name, I will come and be at your side. Every moment you
think of me, I will be with you. I will not refuse another, if I
am with one. That is my promise forever and ever.'

All the women were now smiling with tears in their eyes.
Soon, Krishna was holding each of them in his arms. There were

eight Krishnas, but each queen only saw her own. Each started laughing, crying, kissing and hugging their Krishna.

Krishna was now out of the room, away from his queens. This was how he used to be with gopis when he went away to see Radha. No Gopi realized he was not there.

He still had a lot to do. He collected his bow and arrows. He got out and found Daruka.

'Go and arrange a large sailing ship for a long journey. It will have three people on it. Raja Maya will be there, accompanied by the two women you saw with me yesterday. Look out for Raja Maya and Takshak when they come in their boat. When Raja Maya arrives, take the two women to the sailing ship. I am going to lie down in the green grove with the beautiful mango trees. Bring him there. But just him, no one else. They will all sail tonight.'

ౚౚ

27

Farewell

It was late in the afternoon by the time the boat reached Dwarka. They had been lucky with the wind behind them. Sindhu had been kind, flowing rapidly, while they came down from where Maya had been. Maya was very quiet—he was worried about Raghi and Anuja. Takshak and Shukri tried to divert his mind by pointing to the sites along the way as they were speeding past.

When they finally arrived at Dwarka, Maya immediately saw Raghi and Anuja waiting for him with a chariot. He was much relieved. They hugged each other warmly as if they were meeting each other after eons, although it had only been two days. Shukri immediately embraced Raghi and Anuja as did Takshak.

Daruka said, 'I am to take you to your ship, which is ready to sail. It is fully stocked for your long journey and there are sailors who will steer. I am then to take Raja Maya because Bhagwan Krishna wants to talk to him alone.'

Takshak was astonished.

'What has happened? I was hoping Krishna would be here to receive us and show us Dwarka and Maya Raja would take our leave after some days. This way, he will not be able to see Dwarka at all.'

'My lord, there is nothing to see in Dwarka, but killing and death. Young men are on a rampage and no one is safe. This is why Bhagwan Krishna sent me here to take you safely to your boat. He is waiting to give Raja Maya a message.'

Takshak was mystified, but understood that Krishna wanted to see Maya alone. That was fine with him. He could have shown Dwarka to Raghi and Anuja himself. He had many friends. Now he understood why Krishna had communed with him to bring Maya back.

Their sailing ship was nearby, along the seafront. Daruka helped Raghi and Anuja get down, and Takshak helped Shukri. They told Maya to let Krishna know that they would come and see him tomorrow before sailing back. They knew that Krishna was in some sort of a hurry to see Maya. They let him go.

Daruka decided to skirt the town on his way to the grove behind the palace. He knew that grove well because Krishna often went and rested there. Maya was silent as he began to have forebodings. Dwarka was in flames and Krishna was resting in a mango grove? It did not make sense. What did he want to say to him? When they parted the last time, Krishna had insisted he come and meet him before leaving for home. Then he hurried his departure. Why?

Daruka stopped. He helped Maya off the chariot. In the fading light, Maya saw Krishna lying down comfortably, resting his head on what looked like a cushion, but was a stump of a tree. He was stretched out.

Krishna said, 'Daruka, wait outside while I speak with Raja Maya. He will find you.' Daruka promptly left.

Turning to Maya, Krishna said, 'Welcome, my friend. I wanted to say farewell before you left us.' He got up and hugged Maya. Maya was moved.

'Of course, I had to come. You have shown me so much love that I could not leave your land before saying farewell. But why the hurry? And what has happened to Dwarka?'

'Dwarka is in flames because it has violated dharma. The

young men insulted maharishis and were cursed by them with instant death by killing each other. That is the fate they invited upon themselves.'

'But could you not have intervened and got the curse rescinded? The maharishis have always respected you.'

'This time I did not. For a reason.'

'What was the reason?'

'You.'

'Me? How?'

'Remember, you said to me on the boat that I had let the Aryas die, but shielded the Vrishnis?'

'I was just making an argument against your idea of dharma.'

'No. You pointed out to me that I had failed in upholding dharma. I had favoured my people over the Aryas.'

'So you did not intervene and let them die?'

'Yes. I am grateful to you for putting me on the right path.'

'But I would have saved the Aryas and the Vrishnis if I were you.'

'You are not responsible for upholding dharma. I am.'

'So, what now?'

'You have to do me one more favour. Here is a bow and arrows. I will recline here as if I am asleep. You must shoot an arrow in the sole of my foot.'

'Why would I do that?'

'Because that is the only way I can be killed. You are the only person in all Aryavarta who can kill me.'

'But why do you want to die? Why would I kill you after all the love and respect you showed me?'

'It is because you love me that you must do this. I have a boon that no weapon aimed at my body can kill me. The soles of my feet are the only weak part. No one in Aryavarta can ever aim at the soles of my feet. But you are not from Aryavarta. You are a Mayan. You have to do this one favour, Quetl.'

Maya was thunderstruck.